"KI? WHAT *IS* IT?"

"I don't know," he snapped. "Gaiter, look out!"

Jessie turned. Her boot caught a loose board and sent her sprawling. In the smallest part of a second she saw it happen...the enormous gray shadow sprang past Ki out of the alley. Gaiter stood frozen in the street...his hand snaked to his waist and three quick explosions brightened the night. The thing leaped off the ground with a snarl and slammed him in the chest. Gaiter shrieked...the creature tore at him, shook its great head.

"Oh, God!" Jessie's stomach turned and she quickly looked away. Gaiter's throat was completely gone. His face was twisted in horror...

⟅ WESLEY ELLIS ⟆

LONE STAR

AND THE KANSAS WOLVES

A JOVE BOOK

LONE STAR AND THE KANSAS WOLVES

A Jove Book / published by arrangement with
the author

PRINTING HISTORY
Jove edition / October 1982

ISBN: 0-515-06229-4

Jove books are published by Jove Publications, Inc.,
200 Madison Avenue, New York, N. Y. 10016. The words
"A JOVE BOOK" and the "J" with sunburst are trademarks
belonging to Jove Publications, Inc.

PRINTED IN THE UNITED STATES OF AMERICA

★

Chapter 1

Ki made his way back along the train toward his own compartment. Most of the cars he passed were relatively empty. The few passengers aboard kept to themselves, drowsing in the sultry afternoon or staring straight ahead. There was nothing to see outside, only shimmering waves of heat off the flat Kansas plain. The KP wasn't getting rich on this trip, which didn't surprise Ki at all. Anyone who didn't have to travel would be back home resting in the shade, instead of baking in a fine upholstered oven.

Sometimes a passenger glanced up and gave him a quick, curious look as he passed. Ki was used to that and ignored it. For the most part, he looked no different from a thousand other young men. His suit was a simple blue-gray tweed cut to fit his lean, wiry frame. He wore a twill cotton shirt the color of a pale winter sky, and a plain shoestring tie. A black Stetson and ankle-length Wellingtons completed his wardrobe.

Still, there were differences, if you cared to look for them. His hair was straight and hung to the top of his collar. In the light, it had the blue-black cast of a raven's wing,

1

the sheen of burnished metal. The hair formed a sharp point high in the center of his brow, then swept back abruptly to show the prominent curve of his skull.

It was the eyes, though, that most often caught a stranger's attention. They were a deep, penetrating brown, and seemed to have no whites at all. A small fold of skin close to the lids lifted slightly at the corners to show his Oriental heritage. The high, sharp plane of his cheeks and the quick sweep of his jaw completed the image.

If a man bothered to notice Ki at all, he simply glanced up a moment and looked away. Women, though, let their eyes linger a little longer. Bolder young ladies studied him with open curiosity. The pretty redhead at the end of the car was one of those. She fastened on him the minute he entered the coach, and followed him all the way through. Ki returned the glance but didn't stop. He was interested, but something else had caught his attention.

Two men sat together across the aisle from the girl. Just before Ki passed the middle of the car, they stood and walked casually before him out the door to the platform between the two coaches. Ki came instantly alert. To his trained eye, they telegraphed their purpose in a dozen different ways. A swing of the arm, a slight, almost imperceptible tightening around the mouth. To Ki, their bodies betrayed them with every step they took. The lazy, indifferent manner of the pair told him something else entirely— something they didn't wish him to see.

Part of this was *kime,* the subtle hint of power and purpose the samurai learned to sense in another. Part of it was something else that had no name. The enemies Ki sensed here lacked the fire and strength of fighters with honor. There was a vague hint of darkness, a twisting of the soul that told him what the pair were, what they wanted from him.

Ki left the coach and walked straight for the two. They stood between the swaying cars, blocking his way, making a show of ignoring his presence. They were stocky, hard-

2

faced men, one slightly taller than the other. The tall one wore a Colt Peacemaker under his belt. The other was seemingly unarmed, a fact Ki noted with care.

"Excuse me," he said politely. "I am going to the next car, gentlemen."

The man with the Colt drew a cheroot out of his vest, then turned to Ki as if he'd suddenly appeared out of the air. "Willie, you see anyone tryin' to get by?"

Willie frowned and sniffed the air. "No. But I sure do *smell* something." He looked straight at Ki and grinned broadly. "By God. You know what we got here, Karl? We got us a real yellow nigger."

Karl tried to look pained. "That's a Chinaman, son. One of your gen-yoo-wine chinks. Isn't that right, mister? They call you Ching or Chow or what?"

Willie sniggered at that, and granted Ki another grin.

"You're mistaken," Ki said gently. "I'm not Chinese. I'm half Caucasian and half Japanese."

"Oh, damn, I'm sorry." Karl looked at Willie and frowned. "See now, we was wrong. He ain't a chink-chink at all. He's a Jap-chink." Willie liked that, too.

"I would like to pass, please," said Ki. His breathing was slow and easy, spreading calmness throughout his body. This journey was important to Jessie; he had no wish to call attention to himself or to her with a fight. The pair's insults meant nothing.

Karl's smile suddenly vanished. "You know what?" he said darkly. "I thought chinks was supposed to *build* railroads. I never heard nothin' about 'em *ridin'* on them." His eyes flicked to his friend. "You think maybe Ching here'd be more comfortable closer to the tracks?"

"I sure think he would," Willie agreed.

It was going too far. Ki didn't want it to go further, but he knew there wasn't a chance in hell of getting out of it without trouble. The men wanted it to end this way—Ki had known that from the beginning.

"I would like to get past," he said once again. "Please."

3

Karl liked that. "How 'bout *please* with a little chink dance thrown in?" His fingers edged slowly toward the Colt.

For the first time, Ki answered the man's smile. "Would a Japanese step do?"

"Well, hell, yes it—"

Ki moved. His left hand came up in a blur, fingers thrust out stiffly. The blow struck the gunman at the base of his throat, just above the collarbone. At the same time, his eyes caught the wicked flash of a blade driving straight at his gut. His right hand was already in motion in the *shuto-uchi,* the knife-hand strike. A blade for a blade, thought Ki.

Willie howled and grabbed his shattered wrist. Ki whipped his hand up again and chopped him once across the temple.

The whole encounter had taken less than two seconds. Neither man was quite unconscious, but both were paralyzed with pain and would give him no trouble. They were alive only because he had used just enough force to put them out of action and avoid injury to himself.

Now, though, he had the problem of what to do with them. At any moment, someone was likely to come through the door of either car for a breath of air and find him with two men writhing in pain. He could leave them, and go about his business. Which meant they would surely trouble him again. He could call the conductor and have them locked up until the next stop—but that, too, would call attention to Jessie and himself.

Ki knew the only logical answer was to remove them from the scene. The train was moving at high speed across the flat countryside—which meant they might injure themselves or maybe even break their necks. He stoically accepted the possibility. They had initiated this encounter, and must face the consequences.

Quickly he went through their pockets, then hefted them up one by one and tossed them over the side. A few moments later he threw their weapons far out over the prairie and straightened his jacket. With any luck at all, everyone aboard would be too bored to glance out their windows and see two stout bodies tumbling by.

He opened the door to his own coach and walked to Jessie's compartment, and saw the man sitting beside her. The man said something that amused her, and Jessie laughed. Her green eyes crinkled at the corners, and she tossed a shock of strawberry blonde hair over her shoulders.

Ki disliked the man instinctively, and knew his feelings were only partly due to the stranger's easy manner with Jessie. He was a tall, striking man in his early forties, with an aristocaratic nose and and commanding blue-agate eyes. Silver patches brushed the sides of his temples, tinting a full head of curly black hair. The silver was a perfect match for his expensive, dove-gray suit and dark blue shirt. *Polished* was the word that thrust itself into Ki's mind. The man was entirely too polished, too smoothly honed, for Ki's liking.

Jessie glanced up, saw Ki, and quickly motioned him into the compartment. "Oh, Ki—I'd like you to meet Mr. Torgler. He's going to Roster, same as we are."

"Very pleased to meet you," said Torgler, in a mellifluous voice Ki had fully expected. He thrust out a strong hand, and Ki grasped it. "Miss Starbuck and I were just passing the time. Devilishly hot, isn't it?"

"Yes it is," said Ki. He felt the man's eyes all over him, and took the opportunity to do some searching of his own. Something was there, but it eluded him for the moment. Torgler was good at hiding what he didn't want seen—and that in itself told Ki a great deal.

Torgler stood and nodded at Jessie. "Ma'am. It's been a pleasure. I hope your stay in Kansas is most rewarding."

"Well, thank you, sir," smiled Jessie. "I've truly enjoyed your company." Without another look at Ki, he walked quickly out of the compartment and disappeared.

Ki slid into a seat across from Jessie. Jessie looked at him and raised an inquisitive brow. "Well now. What was all *that* about?"

"All what, Jessie?"

"All right," she grinned, "don't go Oriental on me, Ki. You know very well what."

Ki shrugged. "I don't like the man, Jessie."

"Didn't much care for him myself, but I think he's likely harmless."

"Why?"

"Why what?"

"Why didn't *you* like him?"

Jessie closed one eye in thought. "Oh, he's a little too...what? Confident. Sure of himself. Nothing wrong with that, but Mr. Torgler makes too big a thing of it."

"Ah," Ki brightened. "Exactly."

Jessie studied him closely. "You're going somewhere with this, aren't you?"

"Maybe. Maybe not." He quickly related his encounter with the two men between the cars, and what he'd done with them.

Jessie listened, then let out a sigh. "I don't think there's anything else you could've done, Ki. And as you say, they brought it on themselves." She looked past him, squinting into the late afternoon. "And you think maybe there's a connection, right? That it has something to do with our business?"

"There's no way to tell. This is not the first time I've had to, ah, *explain* my Oriental heritage. And there is no reason to connect those two with Torgler. Except a look I didn't care for. Oh, I did go through their clothing. There was nothing to connect them with our business."

"'Course, if they're mixed up with our European friends, there wouldn't be," Jessie said shortly.

"No, there wouldn't." Ki shook his head. Something about Torgler kept tugging at the back of his mind. Jessie had noticed it too. Ki's old teacher, Hirata, had put it into

6

words long ago, and now Ki remembered. It is easy to spot a bruise on an apple. But what of the fruit that is rotting from the inside out? That was Torgler—or at least it was Ki's impression of the man. But again, there was nothing at all Ki could really put his finger on.

The flat plains of the Kansas heartland flashed by the window, one mile stretching into another. Jessica Starbuck stared at her reflection in the dusty glass and didn't much like what she saw. Not for the first time, she felt that terrible sense of loneliness, the fear that she had bitten off a great deal more than she could chew. Even the loyal Ki, who in many ways knew her and understood her better than anyone else, could do little to help her at moments like this. He would protect her with his life, use his keen sense of danger and almost frightening talents to guard her from harm. In the end, though, she was alone. She was Jessica Starbuck, her father's child and heiress to the vast Starbuck holdings. She had inherited both the power of that title and the awesome responsibility that went with it.

And always, overshadowing all else, was the ever-present specter of those faceless men who would take it all from her—who had ruthlessly murdered her father, and signed her own death warrant at the same time.

Jessie knew the story well, even those parts not another living soul could recount. She had grown up with a part of it, seen it in her father's restless eyes, and heard the final chapter only moments before his death. Alex Starbuck had been a maverick from the start, a man who set his own course and knew what he wanted. Many young men had sailed with Commodore Perry to open the door to Japan. Most had served out their time and come back home with only the memory of that exciting adventure in the Orient. Alex Starbuck came home too—but not for long. He liked what he saw in Japan, and returned to learn more about those isles and their people. Later, when he knew what he needed to know, he returned to San Francisco, sought out

7

a group of wealthy men, and made them a proposition. There were fortunes to be made in that newly opened land. He, Alex Starbuck, could deliver valuable import/export contracts with the Japanese. All he needed was money. He was a persuasive young man, and in time, the money came to him.

Starbuck took another important step in San Francisco. He married a lovely young copper-haired girl named Sarah, a woman who stood by his side all her life as his lover and companion.

Jessie had fond memories of her childhood in San Francisco—memories of her breathtakingly beautiful mother and the big, handsome man who was her father. Those were years when she was showered with presents from Alex Starbuck's Eastern trips—silks, painted fans, and small ivory boxes with tiny cities and people carved in their sides. Better still, there were stories of fierce, scowling warriors, and secret gardens with exquisite lakes and trees—and still more exquisite ladies posed on delicate bridges, like butterflies on a branch.

At the time, Jessica was too young to know the rest of the story—that there were others interested in making their fortunes in the Orient, men from wealthy business cartels in Europe. Always on the alert for ways to extend their holdings, they saw such an opportunity in the successful young American. Money was tight in the late 1850s, and Starbuck was overextended. A group of Prussian businessmen approached him with an offer that seemed made in heaven. They needed Alex's ships for their silk trade, and were willing to sublease them at a staggering profit for Alex. Starbuck, of course, snapped at the offer—and soon learned the reasons behind the generous terms. The Prussians weren't shipping silks at all. Their cargo was Chinese slaves.

Alex tried to fight them, but the experienced Europeans were ready for him. They struck out at the Starbuck interests in the Orient and tried to ruin him, using every weapon they

8

could bring to bear—coercion, bribery, and even murder. And Alex Starbuck struck back...

Jessie sighed and sank back in her seat, listening to the hypnotic rhythm of the rails. From her window she watched the sun falling rapidly over the horizon behind a brilliant array of clouds. The broad, open fields of Kansas seemed greatly out of place with the thoughts that plagued her mind. Sometimes she found it all hard to believe, though she'd heard the tale from her father himself, when Alex Starbuck knew he was dying. It was a terrible, ugly story—nearly impossible to relate to the man himself. Starbuck had fought his enemies from one continent to another. Ships were hijacked and warehouses burned. Treachery was the order of the day, and there were no holds barred. It was a game her father hated, Jessie knew. But he was in it, and there was no getting out.

Finally the war intensified in a manner Starbuck had never imagined. On a trip to Europe, a runaway carriage struck down Sarah and killed her. Starbuck knew it was no accident—he, instead of his wife, had been the target. In a rage that Jessie could still not connect to the kind and gentle man she'd known her father to be, Starbuck took his revenge. He found the man responsible for Sarah's death. They had taken from him, and he would take from them in kind. The old Prussian count had a son, a young man in his twenties. Alex Starbuck, who had never committed a violent act in his life, killed the Prussian's heir with his own hands...

"Jessie?"

She looked up and found Ki watching her. She could hardly make out his face in the gathering dark, but knew what was there. "Yes, Ki?"

"It does no good to go back," he said gently. "It can change nothing."

Jessie forced a laugh. "More Oriental wisdom, old friend?"

"Nothing so grand, I'm afraid. Only words. Things that scatter quickly in the wind, and are likely as useless as brittle leaves."

"No, that's not so at all," she told him, reaching across to touch his hand. "Not true at all, Ki."

Starbuck had told her the rest of the story on his deathbed, his eyes flooded with tears of shame. The murder of his enemy's son was the one act in his life he could never forgive, though he was paying for it dearly.

The old count waited, and finally struck back. His assassins caught Starbuck in a hail of bullets on his own Texas ranch. An eye for an eye, one man's son for another man's wife—and then the man himself.

And it doesn't stop there, Jessie thought grimly. The earth was dark and the gloom seemed to close in around her. *It goes on and on, and there is no way to bring it to an end...*

Chapter 2

In light of his earlier encounter, Ki urged Jessie to let him stay in her compartment for the night. She could curl up under a blanket on one side of the small room, while he kept watch.

"You will be less comfortable," he told her, "but you will be safe."

"I don't think there'll be any trouble, Ki. Really," said Jessie. "And you'll be right next door."

Ki pushed the point, but in the end Jessie won out—promising to keep a revolver handy and pound the wall if she needed help.

After a quick dinner she didn't enjoy, she let the porter make up the room and locked the door behind him. She knew, of course, that it made little difference whether Ki was with her, or just behind a wall. Even when there was little chance of trouble, he'd be on guard. Ki slept, but it wasn't what she called sleep at all; at the slightest hint of danger, his mind and body would be instantly alert. She didn't pretend to understand how he did this; she simply accepted it for what it was. It was a part of Ki. A part of *kakuto bugei,* the true samurai way. And a samurai, she knew, was as likely to let himself fall into a deep, snoring sleep on guard as he was to dig for worms with his precious *katana* longsword.

Jessie turned the light down low, slipped out of her tweed jacket and skirt, and perched on the bed to remove her stockings and cordovan boots. Standing again, she slid the white silk blouse off her shoulders, unhooked the light chemise underneath, and let it fall about her ankles. She was naked now, except for the red garter holster she wore high on her left thigh. Neither the holster nor the ivory-handled derringer tucked inside did much to hide her charms.

Crossing the small compartment, she caught a quick glimpse of herself in the narrow strip of mirror—a flash of full, uptilted breasts, the curve of a thigh tinted in gold in the soft light. Jessie approved of what she saw, and neither lingered nor turned away from her reflection. Many young women of her day might have blushed at their own sexuality, she knew—but old Myobu, the geisha who had been her father's courtesan in his early days in Japan, and later Jessie's friend, tutor, maid, and almost mother, had taught her better than that. A body was born with its beauty, and the feelings that went with it. Whether she was alone or in the arms of a man, those feelings, for Jessie, were as natural and healthy as breathing.

Turning off the light, she stretched out on the coarse railway sheet, closed her eyes, and listened to the miles clack by. Even though the sun had vanished hours before, the land held on to its heat. The compartment was stuffy and close. She was tempted to raise a window, but then thought better of it. Smoke and cinders from the big Baldwin engine would have filled the room instantly.

"Damn it all, anyway!" she said crossly. Slipping bare legs to the floor, she sat up and glared at the wall. The thoughts of the day still plagued her, and wouldn't let go. She couldn't put the looming shadow of the cartel out of her mind. They were always there—her father's enemies, and now her own. She'd learned a great deal about them since Alex Starbuck's murder; they were bigger and far more frightening than she'd first imagined. It wasn't just the Starbuck empire they wanted. That was only the start. It was the country itself they had their eyes on—a young and burgeoning nation of untold wealth and promise. They wanted that wealth, and would stop at nothing to get it. She and Ki had met them head-on more than once, and knew what they were capable of doing.

Jessie leaned back with a sigh. And now it was likely starting again. Like Ki, she didn't believe his encounter had simply happened—not with the two of them headed for Roster, Kansas, and the problems they'd face there. The message had come to the Starbuck ranch three days before. The Starbuck land offices had financed a number of groups of European immigrants—loaned them the money to get wheat started, in exchange for crop committments. Now those immigrants wanted to back down, sell their land at disastrous prices, and move on fast.

Why? Jessie wondered. They'd come from the Old World to get a new start. What was scaring them off? Instinct, and a few lessons learned the hard way, told her the cartel had its hand in the deal somewhere.

Finally, Jessie drifted off to sleep, but her waking thoughts followed her into dark and fitful dreams...

When Jessie Starbuck entered the diner for breakfast, she earned the admiring glances of every male in the car—and chilly looks from their wives. For the sake of comfort, she'd cast aside her more tailored traveling wear in favor of faded, sky-blue denims and a matching jacket. The wide brown leather belt emphasized the natural slimness of her waist. The denims were scandalously tight, and when Jessie moved down the aisle to the click of her boots, the motion caused lovely things to happen to her firm bottom.

She was aware of the whispers in her wake, and ignored

them. Trailing a wealth of riotous, strawberry-blonde hair over her shoulders, she made her way to the table Ki was holding. The strain of the day before and a nearly sleepless night should have left her drawn and depressed. Instead, her stubborn Starbuck heritage had come to the fore, and she'd traded the mood for a saucy and impish air. She would *not* give in to her troubles, and by God, anything that got in her way would wish it hadn't!

"Morning," she greeted Ki cheerily. "Slept well, I hope?"

"As well as you, I'm sure," he said, raising his brow a bare quarter-inch.

Jessie got the message and stuck out her tongue. "All right, so I didn't. And you didn't, either." She gave a light shrug and glanced out the window. *"Beautiful* day, Ki. Just marvelous!"

"Yes, it is quite pleasant," he agreed. Her cheery mood pleased him, and he held back a smile. Samurai discipline was certainly not Jessie's way, but sometimes she showed a remarkable ability to be what she wanted to be—in spite of what was going on around her. "I've ordered eggs, ham, and muffins," he said solemnly. "Will that be sufficent?"

"Don't be cute," warned Jessie. "Not till I've downed some of that good railroad coffee."

Ki hailed a waiter, who immediately filled their cups. Jessie made a pleasant sound in her throat and went after the scalding liquid.

"Oooooh, my dear! My goodness *gracious!"*

Jessie paused and stared, the cup halfway to her lips. The chubby little lady waddled down the aisle toward the table, swinging her purse in delight.

"Child, if you are not the *image* of my daughter, Lou Ann? Lord, I *never!* Is this seat taken, honey?"

"Uh—"

"Oh, good!" She slapped a hand to her ample breasts and sank down across from Jessie. "Just hate to eat alone. You know?" She blinked through spectacles that made her eyes look as big as small moons. "Don't tell me now. No, wait, let me get it m'self." She tapped a finger on her teeth. "You ain't a Wheeler, are you? No, the Wheelers don't run to pretty hair, and you sure got that." Suddenly her eyes lit up and she stabbed the air with her hand. "A *Morrison.* Now that's it, tell me I'm wrong, child."

"I'm terribly sorry." Jessie grinned and shook her head. "I don't think I'm either one. Guess I'm mostly a Starbuck."

The woman's face fell. "Oh, dear, you just *got* to be kin somewhere. Lord, if you an' Lou Ann was sittin' side by side, it'd be like tryin' to tell one pea from another. 'Course, she's a little stouter." She cackled and shook at the thought. "A *little* stouter, I say. That and then some! All us Wheeler girls take to fat. Runs in the family." She leaned toward Jessie and frowned. "You suppose they got tea on this train, 'stead of coffee, dear? You get real *nice* tea on the Union Pacific. Don't know why the other lines don't do it. Now, when I come into Denver last May—no, I'm tellin' a lie. Was it May, or last part of April? Had to be May, 'cause Lottie was expectin' her first and that'd be May. Lord, I said to Lou Ann—"

Jessie rolled her eyes and cast a furtive glance at Ki. Ki, though, pretended great interest in the steaming hot muffins and crisp fresh ham arriving at the table. *Coward,* Jessie thought ruefully. *Some samurai you are!*

Jessie couldn't fault the old lady—she was doing what old ladies did. It just wasn't the right morning to hear about overweight daughters named Lottie and Lou Ann. Jessie picked at her food, nodding now and then at her uninvited guest. At least, she thought drearily, no answers were required—just a nod in the right places.

Glancing up, she saw her acquaintance of the day before move past to the front of the diner. Torgler was sporting a handsomely cut black suit, a plum-covered vest, and a soft ivory shirt. The black pearl pin in his blue ascot was just the right size—neither too small nor overly pretentious. The man ignored Ki, nodded politely at Jessie, and vanished behind her.

Jessie ground her teeth and muttered under her breath. Torgler made a real show of being a gentleman, but she hadn't missed the way his eyes brushed over her breasts. There was nothing wrong with a man's admiration. Jessie welcomed it, and more than once gave back as good as she got. Torgler, though, was a sneak—not man enough to hang an honest smile on to his look.

"—Lou Ann's first young'un. Lord, no, you'd think Jimmy come from a *whole* different family. He wasn't no more like—why, what's wrong, girl?"

"Nothing, nothing at all," Jessie said lightly. She pushed back her chair and stood. "Be right back. Just catching a quick breath of air." She shot a look at Ki and darted down the aisle before the old lady could get her engine going again.

The woman looked at Ki, a little frown creasing her brow. "That girl is *not* well," she said darkly. "Not well *at* all. I got two of my own, and Lord, don't I know the signs!"

"I'm certain she is all right," Ki assured her. "Truly."

"Huh!" She sniffed at Ki and lifted her great bottom off the chair. "What's a *man* goin' to know 'bout sufferin'? Think I can't see *sick* when it's starin' me in the face? Poor dear child!"

Ki watched her wander off after Jessie. She looked for all the world like a feather mattress loosely bound in baling wire—with a tuft of gray down spouting out the top. Poor Jessie, indeed! Ki suppressed a grin and went back to his breakfast.

Jessie stood between the two coaches and took a deep breath of cool morning air. Good God, the woman could talk the ears off a mule! One more word about Lottie and the kids and—the door opened behind her and Jessie turned abruptly.

"Oh, *there* you are, my dear!"

"What?" Jessie blinked and bit her lip. "Listen, it's—nice of you to worry, but I'm really all right. Honest."

16

"I'm so glad to hear that, Miss Starbuck." The pleasant smile faded. "Now get back away from that door—fast!"

"What? Hey, now—"

"*Move* it, sister!" A hand slipped into the folds of her shawl and came out with a large Smith & Wesson. Jessie stared and backed off. The thick spectacles were suddenly gone, and so was the crackly old voice. The former grandmother leveled the revolver and thumbed back the hammer. "Miss Starbuck, you got a choice," she said evenly. "Jump off this train with your heart still pumping, or go off dead. Decide right now. Don't make a hell of a lot of difference to me, one way or the other."

Jessie looked into the cold, slate-gray eyes and knew she meant it. "Mind telling me what this is all about? If it's a robbery, you—"

"Damn it," the woman blurted, "I got no time to *talk!*" Jessica saw cords tighten in the lady's wrist, and knew the action came from a finger squeezing back on a trigger. God, the woman didn't intend to wait for an answer, she meant to kill her then and there!

"All *right*," blurted Jessie, "I'll jump, damn it, if that's what you—" Jessie took one step toward the door, twisted at the waist, and kicked out hard with the toe of her right boot. The motion brought her body around at an angle, left shoulder slanting at the floor, left hand sweeping up fast under the woman's wrist. Foot and hand found their targets at once. The woman shrieked and came off her feet. A white blossom of fire exploded near Jessie's ear and singed her hair as the Smith & Wesson punched a neat hole in the roof. Jessie hung on and followed her assailant to the floor. The woman lashed out with her feet and bruised Jessie's ribs with her free hand. Jessie gritted her teeth and took it, fighting to keep the pistol out of her face. The woman was strong, and nowhere close to finished. Jessie tried to remember everything Ki had tried to teach her. She buried her head in the woman's shoulders and let the tight fists pound away and tear at her clothes. Nothing counted now

17

except keeping that revolver aimed in some other direction. Again and again she slammed the thing hard against the steel floor. The woman cursed, came up off the floor, and bit Jessie's ear.

Jessie bellowed, jerked over fast, and shoved the woman's head into the wall. The gun fell free. The woman broke loose and went after it on all fours. Jessie leaped, determined to get there first.

Suddenly something swept past her, scooped the woman easily off the floor, and wrapped strong arms about her waist. Jessie shook her head and came to her feet. The woman screamed and cursed like a sailor, churning her legs in the air.

"We have a very active old lady here," Ki grinned. "Very strong for her age."

Jessie pulled her torn silk blouse together as well as she could and scooted around to Ki's side, carefully avoiding the kicking legs. "A little *too* active, if you ask me. And not all that old, either." Jessie reached up and yanked off the iron-gray wig. A full head of shiny auburn hair sprang free and tumbled over the woman's shoulders.

"Damn you, leave me alone!" she screamed, twisting under Ki's steel grip.

"Granny, you've got real pretty hair under there," said Jessie. "And I'll bet there's a face somewhere to go with it." Using an edge of the woman's shawl, she scrubbed the weathered features with a vengeance. Years fell away like magic, along with overgrown brows and well-applied wrinkles. Jessie stepped back and took a look.

The girl glared. "You satisfied?"

"I guess so. Ki, she isn't a day older than I am. And I'll bet there's a lot more cotton than fat under that gown. Have you ever seen her before?"

"Ah, yes—I am afraid so," Ki said dryly. "I saw her yesterday. She was sitting across the aisle from the men who attacked me."

Jessie sighed and shook her head. "Miss, if you're half

as smart as I think you are, you know you're in an awful lot of trouble. You want to be helpful or try the other way?"

"Go to hell, lady!" the girl snarled.

Jessie exchanged a quick glance with Ki. "If you know who I am, you likely know my friend here, too. He can touch a certain point on your neck and everything'll kind of go black for a while. Of course, if he doesn't do it just right . . ."

"Hey, now, look—" For a moment, the girl went pale. "You want to tell me anything?"

"I . . . got nothing to say. Whatever you do to me!" Her eyes were still bold and determined, but her voice lacked some of the bravado of a moment before. Jessie had no intention of asking Ki to use his arts on the girl, and Ki well knew it. The girl, however, wasn't all that sure.

"Why don't we start off with something easy?" Jessie suggested. "What's your name?"

"It's . . . Lucy Jordan," the girl said quickly.

Likely something she made up on the spot, thought Jessie. "Fine, Lucy. Now I know this wasn't your idea. Who put you up to it?"

Lucy laughed in her face. "A man named Smith, lady. It always is—'less it's Jones sometimes!"

"Is he on this train?" Ki put in. "Can you point the man out?"

"Sure." Lucy shrugged and gave him a wink over her shoulder. "If he's wearin' a big brown envelope with some fat bills in it, I'll know him right off. That's all I ever seen of him."

"She's probably telling the truth," sighed Jessie. "She's good, and the cartel hires only the best. I expect it happened the way she said. Somebody knows somebody who knows how to contact the right person, and nobody can trace the business back to the beginning." She looked straight at Lucy Jordan. "Is that how it works, friend?"

Lucy shrugged, doing her best to show a lack of interest. "Listen, Miss Starbuck. Don't take it personal-like, all

19

right? Hell, it's just a job. I got nothing against you."

Jessie met the girl's eyes and felt a chill touch the back of her neck. She was young, and almost a striking beauty. She was also a professional assassin, and most likely meant just what she said. Jessica Starbuck or anyone else was a job and nothing more—a person who should have been cold meat right now, instead of standing up, talking to her killer.

"Thanks," she told the girl calmly. "Knowing that sure makes me feel a whole lot better."

★

Chapter 3

If Jessica Starbuck had simply wanted to *see* Roster, Kansas, she could have accomplished that without stepping off the train. The whole town was visible from the window of her compartment. Past the one-room depot was Main, fronted on either side by two saloons, the hotel and livery, and half a dozen other squat structures baking in the sun. From the tracks to the last building in town was a bare two hundred yards. After that, a person was either leaving town or just coming in.

Jessie stepped off the Kansas Pacific seconds before the squealing brakes brought the train to a halt. She was calm and relaxed now—her encounter with Lucy Jordan had taken care of that. There were no more uncertainties about the way things were. The enemy had shown his hand and the battle lines were drawn.

"Hey, look." Jessie touched Ki's arm and nodded to the right. "There's our friend getting off now. Lord, Ki, I *guess* it is, anyhow. That girl is sure some granny!"

"Yes," Ki said soberly, "indeed she is." He followed Jessie's glance three coaches down, where a pair of con-

21

ductors were marching Lucy Jordan past the tracks toward the town marshal's office. Without the heavy cotton padding of her disguise, she was truly a sight worth seeing. No one in Roster was going to mistake her for an old lady now. She wore a light blue, form-fitting gown laced with narrow white ribbon. The hot Kansas sun made rivers of light in her hair, turning amber to brass. Lucy held her head high and proud, stalking well ahead of her guards. Her long, determined stride emphasized the slender lines of her body, and an ample supply of womanly curves.

Ki pulled his eyes away and found Jessie grinning. "Not hard to guess what you're thinking," she said lightly. "They're not making assassins like they used to, are they?"

"No. I suppose this is true." He cleared his throat and squinted past Lucy down the street. "Are we going to find Tom Bridger now, or go first to the hotel?"

"Both and neither, I guess. I'd like to follow Lucy over to the jail. You and I are the only ones who can tell the law what happened back there. We ought to get it settled." Jessie frowned past the tracks. "That girl's dangerous, Ki. I'd just as soon make sure she's not running around loose somewhere."

Ki picked up their two leather valises and followed Jessie past the depot and the first saloon to the town marshal's office. The scene inside the office set her green eyes blazing. Lucy Jordan was perched in a chair looking scared, and all of fifteen years old. Her hands were crossed primly in her lap, a gesture that somehow managed to press her young breasts up high. Her big doe eyes were locked on the marshal, and tears streamed down her cheeks. The marshal wasn't even listening to the trainmen. He was having Lucy for supper, and starting on dessert.

When the front door slammed, the lawman jerked around, irritation crossing his weathered features. "All right, damn it, who do you think you—" He got a look at Jessie and his eyes went wide. One breathtaking beauty in Roster was an event. Two were a little more than he could handle.

"Uh—yes, ma'am?" he grinned sheepishly. "I'm Marshal Gaiter. What can I do for you?"

"You can start by putting your eyes back in your head," Jessie said coolly. "After that, we can get down to business, Marshal."

"Uh—well, sure . . ." The lawman shuffled his worn boots on the wide-plank floor. He blushed hotly. "You like a chair, Miss—"

"Starbuck. Jessica Starbuck. And this is my friend, Ki."

The marshal blinked. "Are you *that*—"

"Right. *That* Starbuck." She nodded to the conductors. "These two gentlemen tell you what happened on the train?"

"They was starting to. Only I can't hardly believe this pretty little chile—"

"Believe it," snapped Jessie. "This *child* tried to kill me. With this."

She reached behind her, pulled open her valise, and tossed the Smith & Wesson at the marshal.

"I never even saw that awful thing before!" bawled Lucy.

"Shut up," said Jessie. Reaching further into the satchel, she dumped the cotton-padded gown, patterned shawl, several tins of makeup and powder, and a bristly gray wig on the floor. "Here's her grandma suit. You'll need it at the trial." She looked at the two conductors. "If you make out some statements before you leave town, I'd be grateful. Guess you need to be getting back, if that's all right with the marshal here?"

"Yeah, sure," Marshal Gaiter grunted. He cast a leary eye at Lucy Jordan. "I'm real disappointed in you, young lady. Damned if I'm not."

"None of this is true," pouted Lucy. "Not a word of it, sir. Just 'cause she's a rich lady an' I'm poor—"

"Uh-huh." The marshal's hard face softened. "Well now, I reckon you'll have a chance to tell your side." Reluctantly he led Lucy to a cell past the rear door of his office, and then rejoined Jessie and Ki. He was a gaunt, weathered man with a tobacco-stained beard. When he moved, he took time

23

planning his route, and Jessie guessed he'd gotten the job because there wasn't much to it, and nobody else in Roster wanted it.

"You be in town a while, Miss Starbuck? Reason I'm askin' is, Roster's not all that big to keep a judge busy full time. Don't know when we'll get around to having a trial." He looked over his shoulder and made a face. "Don't know what I'm going to do with *her,* if we get a couple of drunks or something. Hell, I only got one cell."

"I wouldn't worry," Jessie said blandly. "Lucy won't hurt them unless she gets her hands on a weapon. Oh, I almost forgot," she added, giving the lawman her best smile. "You can help me if you will. I have some contacts here, but I know the marshal has his finger on what's *really* happening. You know?"

The old lawman swelled at Jessie's remark. "Why, I'll sure do what I can."

"Good." Jessie leaned forward on her chair. "I'm here on business concerning the new group of farmers in your county. Do you know them at all? The immigrants from Europe?"

The marshal shrugged and scratched his ear. "Know *of* 'em. What there is to know, which ain't a lot. They're a peaceful bunch. Don't cause any trouble."

"Do you know any of them personally? They must come in town to buy supplies and things."

"Most folks do, but these is some different. Don't buy much of anything, what I hear. Or get into Roster, either. Stick pretty much to themselves."

"And you don't know *any* of them by name?" Jessie persisted.

"Don't have any cause to," Gaiter said bluntly. "Isn't any of 'em got in trouble. Have their own little settlement out to Firelick Creek, and a kinda...*elder,* or somethin', to keep the peace." The marshal shrugged and cleared his throat. "Don't hold much with foreigners myself, but—" He stopped abruptly and looked at Ki. "No offense, of

24

course, mister. I will say those folks tend to their own business."

Jessie looked down at her boots, and then back to the marshal. "Does anyone bother *them?*"

"Huh?" The marshal closed one eye. "You mean folks 'round here? Naw. Nothing out there to bother. Why'd you think that?"

Jessie stood quickly. "I'm very grateful, Marshal Gaiter. Thank you for your time. Where's Tom Bridger's place? Right down the street, I guess?"

The marshal pulled himself together and gave her a curious look. "Damn, that's right, ain't it? Bridger did work for Starbuck, didn't he?"

"What?" Jessie caught the man's words and frowned. "You said *did* work, marhsal. As far as I know—"

The marshal stopped her with a hand and walked past Jessie to the door. "Tom's place is straight down on this side of the street. But you ain't going to find him there, Miss Starbuck. He's dead. Shot down last night some time. Found him this morning behind the Morgan Dollar."

"He's *dead?*" Jessie's face flooded with anger. "Damn, Ki!" She turned on Gaiter. "Do you know who killed him?"

"Nope." The marshal shook his head. "Likely never will, either. Someone just come up to him and poked a Greener shotgun in his belly and pulled the trigger. Didn't hardly make any noise." He cleared his throat and set his lips. "Made a helluva mess, though. Whoever it was took Tom's watch, and whatever money he had on him."

"Of course," Jessie said evenly. "A back-alley robbery."

"Looks like it." Gaiter frowned at Jessie's expression. "Why? You think it was somethin' else?"

"No, I'm sure it wasn't . . ." said Jessie.

"There's only one reason they'd kill him," she said outside. "Tom's the one who alerted us to this business in the first place. He knew something about what the cartel's up to here, Ki. Something he didn't want to put in a telegram."

25

"Most likely," Ki agreed. "Or they simply killed him as an extra warning to us. They are quite capable of that."

"I won't argue the point," Jessie said flatly. "Only I don't think that's it. Tom knew more than he was saying, or he wouldn't have rung the bell on Roster." She sighed and squinted down the street. "Why don't you go on over to the hotel and get us settled in? I'm going to walk down and see if any of Bridger's people know anything. It's a long shot, but it's worth a try. Then maybe we can ride out to that settlement before dark." She caught Ki's look and shot him a grin. "Hey, I'll be all right, old friend."

"Perhaps Tom Bridger thought so too."

Jessie raised an eyebrow. "They caught him at night in the dark. Nothing's going to happen in the middle of Roster, Kansas, in daylight." She glanced down the bright empty street. "Doesn't look to me like much ever has."

"Probably not," Ki said flatly. "But they haven't had Jessica Starbuck here before."

Jessie laughed. "You make me sound like trouble."

"I don't think I will answer that. In the interest of good relations."

Tom Bridger's place was at the far end of town, Roster's largest building. Henderson Implements sold everything a man needed to go into farming: plows, seed, harvest machines and tools, and parts to fit anything that broke. And if a man didn't have a good place to sink his plow, the Green River Land Company, with offices above the store, would help him find one. Both the Henderson and Green River operations were examples of Alex Starbuck's ability to see a need and fill it. Starbuck's combined implement and land establishments were scattered all over the fertile Midwest. Managers like Tom Bridger kept the stores well stocked by rail from company warehouses in Kansas City, Omaha, and a half-dozen other major centers, and did a thriving land-office and crop-futures business. These enterprises did a great deal more than increase profits for the company; like townships with a solid bank behind them, they played a big part in ensuring the community's survival from year to year.

Jessie was well aware of the way the business worked, and of Tom Bridger's part in it. She knew, too, even before she talked with Bridger's employees, that they'd be totally unaware of the true reason behind his murder. Still, it was a thing she had to do. As she expected, the clerks and other employees were shocked by the boss's death, and thought something ought to be done about the increasing lawlessness in Kansas...

Jessie left that dead end behind her and walked back to the hotel to find Ki. There were a lot more people on the street now, most of them men. She could feel their eyes as she passed, but paid them no mind.

The men looked, but kept their peace. Jessica Starbuck was a real beauty, they decided, but there was something about her that made them forget their usual catcalls and whistles. She was a puzzle they weren't real sure how to handle. All woman for certain—soft, slender, and a pleasure to watch. But at the same time, she walked like a lady who might meet a man face to face and look him right in the eye. They didn't know many women like that, and weren't sure they cared to. Still, she was by-God worth walking outdoors to look at. No question at all about that...

Ki quickly arranged for rooms at the Roster Hotel, dropped off his satchel and Jessie's, and walked next door to the Great Atlantic Saloon. The name seemed out of place on that flat Kansas plain, but Ki decided that was probably the whole idea.

At the long wooden bar, he ordered a beer he didn't want. When he drank at all, he preferred good Scotch whisky. The Atlantic barkeep had likely never heard of any such drink, and Ki wasn't about to ask.

Half a dozen midday drinkers were scattered about, and all pretended to ignore him. Ki knew they were well aware of who he was—that he was the peculiar-looking Oriental

27

who'd come in on the Kansas Pacific with Jessica Starbuck. He was certain, too, that there were as many fanciful opinions about what he was doing with such a beauty as there were customers in the room. Moreover, Ki's appearance gave the other drinkers something to think about. While he was dressed the same as most every other man there, in worn denims and plain cotton shirt, he wore no gunbelt, as some did, and only a pair of rope-soled cloth slippers in lieu of the heavy working footwear—boots or high-topped shoes—favored by most men of the region. Unless he was traveling by train and the occasion demanded more formal attire, Ki seldom wore boots or shoes. His training had toughened his feet into lightning-swift, iron-hard weapons, and at the same time had made them almost as sensitive as a second pair of hands. To encase these instruments in tightly bound, cumbersome packages of heavy leather would have been foolish.

There was a fly-specked window to Ki's left that gave a clear view of Main. As he stood at the bar, the window brought him a scene he found interesting. Torgler, their well-attired traveling companion, walked hurriedly down the street with a shorter, less resplendent friend. Whatever the two were discussing, Ki noted that the friend was clearly getting the worse end of the conversation. He was catching pure hell for something, and Ki would have given much to know what it was.

"You *drink* beers, mister, or just collect 'em?"

"What?" Ki turned slightly to see the girl standing behind him. She was young, a girl with a slender, almost delicate figure. Wheat-colored hair framed an upturned nose and a fragile smile. Her eyes were enormous, a startling shade of green sprinkled with bright flecks of gold. They gave her a look of continual curiosity and surprise, and Ki found it hard to pull his gaze away.

"I'm a slow drinker," he said finally, taking a sip to show her.

"If you was to buy *me* one, maybe yours'd go faster." She showed him a lazy smile and sidled up to him. Her

28

gown was cut low, the bodice consisting of faded red feathers that had seen better days. In spite of her willow-slim frame, Ki noted that her breasts were firm and well formed.

"I'd be glad to buy you a beer," he told her, signaling the bored barkeep. "You rather have something else?"

"No, that's—that's fine." She flashed him a smile with her eyes. "I'm Ruby. You goin' to be in town long?"

"Hard to say. As long as our business takes."

"*Our* business?" She raised a curious brow. "Oh, sure. I *did* notice you come in with her. Real pretty lady. She your girl?"

"Miss Starbuck is my employer," Ki said evenly. "And a friend."

"Oh. Well, of course..." Ruby glanced at the ceiling, and Ki made no effort to correct what she was thinking. "If you *were* goin' to be here some," she said slowly, "might be you and me could—well, get acquainted, maybe..."

Ki grinned. The girl had intrigued him from the beginning, and the more he watched her, the more she stirred the growing warmth in his loins. Those startling green eyes were a bold, wanton invitation. At the same time, her voice was almost shy, hesitant—as if she were afraid he might take her up on her offer. It was a contrast he found more than a little exciting.

"I don't see any reason why we shouldn't get better acquainted," he told her. "Do you?"

"Really?" Her eyes sparkled with delight. She glanced quickly over her shoulder at the stairs that led to the second floor. "You think—right now'd be a good time?"

"I can't think of any better time," he said.

The room was small and comfortable; there was a dresser with a bowl and a pitcher, and a bed with a big feather mattress and a bright patterned quilt. A heavy shade kept the harsh summer sun out of the room.

"You like a drink?" she asked him. "I've got a bottle up here if you like."

"No, thank you," said Ki. He crossed the room and put

29

his hands on her waist. She was so slender there, he could almost reach around her. When he bent to kiss her, she gave a little sigh and closed her eyes. Ki explored the warmth and sweetness of her mouth, letting his tongue caress each small and secret hollow. Ruby responded with a hunger of her own, drinking in his kisses. She guided his lips where she wanted them to be, showing him the way with tiny moans and sighs.

Ki let his mouth touch her cheeks and her nose and her eyes, then trail down the column of her throat. A vein pulsed in her neck. His fingers loosened her bodice, and Ruby reached up eagerly to help. When her breasts were bare, she slipped the hooks at her waist and let the gown whisper to the floor.

Ki stood back and looked at her. Ruby caught his expression and gave him a mischievous grin, well aware of exactly what he wanted. Stepping back lightly, she clasped her hands behind her, resting them in the cleft of her hips. The action gave her breasts a saucy tilt, and deepened the hollow just beneath her ribs. Gazing at him from under a veil of tousled hair, she looked for all the world like a little girl caught in the act—doing all the things she wasn't supposed to do. Ki knew she was well aware of what she was doing. It was the same startling contrast he'd seen below in the bar—provocative, hesitant, and overwhelmingly exciting.

"You like what you see?" she whispered.

"Yes. Very much."

"Then maybe you'd better have some, huh?"

"The idea had occurred to me."

Ruby laughed, flopped on the bed on her stomach, and twisted around to face him. Ki slipped quickly out of his clothes. The big green eyes never left him; they touched him all over, followed him intently with a gaze he could almost feel. Her mouth opened slightly, lips full and lazy. She watched him in wonder, never speaking to him at all, saying all she wanted to say with her eyes. He cupped her small breasts in his hands, kissing the dusky nipples until they rose into hard little points. She was terribly sensitive there, and in a moment just the touch of his tongue set her trembling against him.

Ki let his hands trail lightly over her belly, down to the delicate silken nest between her legs. Ruby moaned, lifting her thighs up to greet him. Her fingers moved shyly down his body, almost afraid of what she might find.

"Oh!" A cry escaped her lips; she touched his swollen member, grasped it softly in her fist, and guided it gently inside her. Ki felt the vibrant heat of her body, the warm and fragile flesh pressing around him. He thrust himself eagerly into that warmth; her legs whispered about him, urging him even deeper. Her arms found his back and raced to his hips. Ki thrust harder, no longer afraid the slender body would break beneath him. Ruby caught the rhythm of his love, matched it with her body and the quick little explosions of her breath.

Ki felt himself climbing toward an intense, almost unbearable peak of pleasure. Ruby gasped. Her body trembled and jerked against him in an uncontrollable spasm of joy. She cried out, threw back her head, and laughed as he surged free inside her . . .

"Think I'll ever see you again?" she asked him.

"I don't know," he said. "Sometimes people come together again. I hope we do that, Ruby. You are a treasure I won't forget."

"Honestly?"

"Yes. Honestly." He buttoned his shirt and bent to kiss her. She said nothing at all, but simply smiled with her eyes.

Ki slipped a twenty-dollar gold piece on the dresser and left her. He knew it was likely four times more than she'd ever get in a place like Roster. Paying to love a woman was a thing he didn't wholly understand. Still, it was the path the girl had chosen, and he had meant what he said. He wouldn't soon forget her.

31

★

Chapter 4

The land was flat and barren for a good three miles or so out of Roster. Then the narrow dirt road snaked into gently rolling hills dotted with small clusters of trees. The trees looked tempting with their inviting pools of shade, but Jessie and Ki kept to the road.

"They didn't know anything, and of course I didn't figure they would," Jessie sighed. "Maybe Bridger wrote something down somewhere, but I kind of doubt it."

"No." Ki shook his head and squinted into the sun. "It is as we said before. What he could tell us, he kept in his head."

"Not figuring he wouldn't be here to deliver it in person," Jessie finished. She paused, batting at an angry green fly circling the head of her horse. "Damn! They're a jump ahead of us, Ki. And nobody's being real subtle, are they? They must want that wheat land real bad. I wonder what they've told the settlers to get 'em so itchy to sell—and lose money in the bargain?"

Ki didn't answer. He was thinking about Torgler, seeing him on the streets of Roster with his friend. A man like that wouldn't turn an eye in San Francisco or Denver. But he didn't belong in Roster. Not unless he was doing exactly what Ki figured he was doing...

"Good grief, Ki—can you imagine?" Jessie reined in her horse and peered down into the narrow valley. "Looks like we just rode out of Kansas into the far end of Europe!"

Jessie was right. The settlement looked nothing at all like an American town. The immigrants had clung to their Old World customs and taken little from their adopted land. Instead of scattering their houses over the limitless slopes of grass, the small, sod-roofed dwellings were huddled close together, one wall nearly butting against the next. Early-evening cookfires brought the smell of some strong, spicy soup wafting up the hill. Late shadows stretched across the valley, and to Ki, the shaggy-roofed structures looked like big lazy animals bunched together for the night.

Jessie and Ki made their way down the slope to the village. In the east, vast fields of wheat blazed like gold in the late summer sun. A little distance off, a dark line of trees showed there was water nearby.

"Ki..." Jessie pulled in her horse and pointed curiously off the trail. "Look there. What do you suppose that is?"

Ki glanced at the lone fencepost rammed into the earth. "Flowers of some kind," he muttered to himself, then slid off his mount and walked to the post. A large, intricately woven wreath was hung from a single nail driven into the wood. Ki snapped off a few of the white blossoms and brought them back to Jessie. "Wolfsbane," he told her. "I have seen the plant before. It's poisonous, by the way."

Jessie took one of the flowers, looked at it, and shrugged. "Some kind of custom, I guess."

Ki mounted up and followed her down the hill. Now he could see that there were more of the posts, scattered in a rough circle about the perimeter of the village. Each held one of the pale, flowery wreaths.

Several of the settlers spotted them coming, stopped what

34

they were doing, and watched the pair approach. Jessie waved a greeting, but no one waved back. There was a small, open common in the center of the village, and she urged her mount in that direction. A group of men clad in baggy gray smocks and trousers were gathered there, and one stepped forward to meet her. Jessie smiled. The short, white-bearded old man met her greeting without expression and set his stolid frame directly in her path.

"What is it you want?" he said roughly. Hard blue eyes flicked from Jessie to Ki. "Is nothing here to see. You ride on now."

Jessie exchanged a quick look with Ki. "We need to talk to whoever's in charge. Oh, yes. The *elder*, isn't it?"

"I am in charge," the old man said curtly. "What is it you want, girl?"

"My name is Jessica Starbuck," Jessie told him. "And I—"

"Huh? *You?*" The man blinked and stood up straight. He turned to his fellows, and his stony features split in a weathered grin. Jessie caught her name several times in the rapid, throaty speech, and heard it passed through the crowd.

The bearded man strode forward and thrust out a stubby hand. "Get down, please, Miss Star-book. Excuse the very bad manners, yes? You are mos' welcome here!"

Jessie took his hand, and the man made a courtly show of helping her off the horse. She introduced Ki, and the fellow greeted him like a lost son and slapped him soundly on the back. Jessie caught the name Gustolf—whatever else came after was unpronounceable and she let it go at that.

Gustolf ushered them quickly through the now-friendly crowd and guided them toward a cottage slightly larger than the rest. Fully half the village tried to follow them inside, but Gustolf sternly waved them away and closed the heavily timbered door behind him.

"All of them you must meet," he said, waving his hand expansively. "That is for later, though. Not now. Now we have a glass of Gustolf's very finest wine in honor of

35

Jeskya—Jess-i-ca—hah! I say it! Jess-i-ca Star-buck and her friend. Sonia! The good wine, and make sure the glasses are all clean!"

Ki decided Gustolf was a lusty old man indeed. The deep lines in his face said he couldn't be a day under seventy, yet the girl he introduced as his daughter was a slender, dark-eyed beauty no more than nineteen or twenty. Her skin was pale olive and honey, so fresh and smooth that it seemed to glow. She greeted her father's guests shyly, then ducked her face under a riot of thick black hair and hurried about her business.

"So." Gustolf raised his glass to Ki and Jessie. "I drink to the Star-buck name, lady." He downed the drink quickly and wet his lips. "I . . . read about your father." He looked at the table and shook his head. "It is bad. I am sorry. He was a good man, and we owe him much here."

"Thank you," said Jessie. "I appreciate your thoughts." The wine was sharp but slightly sweet. It left a delicate, fruity taste on her lips. The wine, the dusty amber bottle, and old Gustolf himself blended easily into the somber, Old World mood of the cottage. The few pieces of furniture present were dark and massive, heavily carved with thick leaves and twisted vines. Faded icons of painted and gold-leafed wood with candles mounted beneath them hung about the walls, along with a pair of crossed, crescent-shaped blades that Jessie sensed were far older than anything else in the house. In spite of the sultry summer evening, a fire was crackling in the big stone fireplace. And, to add to the unwanted heat, Sonia was cooking over an enormous black and silver stove that filled one whole side of the room. It was clearly a family treasure, one that had been shined and polished through several generations.

"Gustolf . . ." Jessie leaned toward the old man over the table. "We came out here because we heard you were having some problems. If there's anything we can do to help . . ."

"What?" Gustolf came suddenly alert. "What problems, lady? I do not understand this. What have you heard about my village that I have not?"

36

"I don't really know," said Jessie. "I was hoping you could tell us that." The look in Gustolf's eye told her this was definitely *not* the time to bring up Tom Bridger, and what had happened to him. Gustolf would have known Tom if he knew anybody in Roster, and if he hadn't yet heard about the murder, she figured it could wait. Out of the corner of her eye, she saw that Sonia had stopped work to listen over her father's shoulder.

"What we've heard," Jessie went on, "is that you've got things going real well here and have a good crop coming in—but that you and your people were thinking about selling out now and moving on somewhere else. I don't understand that."

Gustolf looked down at his stubby hands. "I . . . have shame, Miss Jessica. You think we are not grateful for what you have done, yes? I do not blame you for this."

"Oh, please . . ." The old man looked so pained that Jessie reached out instinctively and took his hands. "Look, I don't set myself up to judge what you or anyone else wants to do with what they have. I don't figure that's any of my business. If something's *wrong* here, though, maybe it does concern me. I guess what I'm asking is why the sudden interest in selling something that looks like it's working out so well? I—"

"Ah, business!" Gustolf made a face, pulled himself up quickly, and held out his palms. "It is bad luck to talk business on an empty stomach." He forced a broad grin and filled the glasses again. "You stay and have supper. *Then* we talk. All right?"

"Father . . ." Sonia turned on him, her dark eyes curiously strained. "Maybe . . . our guests would rather get back to town. It will be dark when we finish supper . . ."

"No, no, they will stay," Gustolf said firmly. Jessie caught the silent message that passed between them. "It is all right, Sonia, eh? Go about your business, girl."

Jessie started to speak, but decided against it. Instead, she sipped her wine and looked at the old man, trying to read whatever it was that lay just behind his eyes. Something

37

was definitely there, but he'd hidden it too well for her to see.

Jessie wanted to get Ki aside to see if he could make any sense out of Gustolf's behavior and Sonia's obvious reluctance to have them around. Gustolf, though, gave them no chance to be alone, and stood firm in his resolve to avoid any talk more serious than the various merits of the wines of Central Euorpe. He seemed to have endless information on the subject, and told Jessie and Ki that in the old country he'd been a master winemaker.

"Why did you leave all that?" Ki asked politely. "A master winemaker is a most distinguished person."

"Pah! Not anymore, he isn't!" Gustolf screwed up his face. "That is all gone now. Over. Behind me. And good riddance too!"

"Now, Father..." Sonia came up and rested a hand on his shoulder. Whatever had disturbed her before seemed to have vanished. "Please don't get him on politics," she said, giving her father a scolding glance. "You will never hear the end of it, Miss Jessica."

"Jessie's just fine, and I would like to hear more."

"Hah, you see?" growled Gustolf. "And what would you know, daughter? You have no respect for an old man."

"You are a fine man, and not old at all. And I have much respect for you." She patted him on the cheek and turned away in a whirl of heavy skirts. "Except when you are being an old fool, of course!" Gustolf reached out to grab for her with a big bearlike paw, but Sonia leaped lightly out of his way. Jessie raised a brow at Ki. Apparently the mood in Gustolf's household had shifted as quickly in one direction as it had in the other.

Ki wasn't sure when either Sonia or her father had had time to invite guests to dinner, but they somehow arrived on schedule. There were two of them: a somber, heavyset man in his fifties named Zascha, and a man of Ki's own age called Feodor. It seemed as if Gustolf had deliberately asked one to offset the other. Zascha was a brooding, sour fellow with a permanent frown between his heavy brows, while Feodor was the other side of the coin. He was a darkly handsome man with a nose like a hawk and a full head of thick, curly hair. A lazy grin curled the corners of his lips, and his black eyes flashed with amusement. At first glance, he seemed a man who might drift through life enjoying its pleasures. Ki, however, saw deeper than that. Feodor's easy manner was deceptive. He knew exactly what was taking place around him. Ki recognized something of himself in the man, as well—he moved slowly, because there was nothing happening that required moving fast.

Ki saw something else too. A single glance at Sonia when Feodor entered the room told him the girl was his for the taking. Feodor answered her look—warmly, but without great interest. On the other hand, his dark eyes rested for a long moment on Jessie. Jessie accepted his glance and gave it back boldly, much to Ki's irritation.

Jessie couldn't remember when she'd had so much to eat. The rich, spicy dishes, aided by a continuous flow of the old man's wine, left her sleepy and a little lightheaded.

Gustolf caught her eye and gave her a wink. "Ah, you like our food and drink, lady? That's good. Very good! Here—you must try a sip of this." He made a small circle with his thumb and forefinger and blew a kiss in the air. "It is exquisite, but a very light and airy wine—"

"No, please!" Jessie laughed and held up a protesting hand. "I'm about to pop right now, Gustolf. Don't know where I·got it, but I must have some Hungarian in me somewhere."

Gustolf blinked in surprise. The gloomy Zascha scowled and shook his head.

"Did I say something wrong?"

Gustolf caught her bewildered expression and laughed. "Is nothing, lady. You could not know, yes?"

"What he's trying to say politely," grinned Feodor, "is that you have insulted him greatly, but he forgives you."

"No, no," Gustolf protested.

"Listen, I'm sorry," Jessie began.

"We're Hungarians," Feodor explained, "as far as the rest of the world sees, but we, ah . . . don't acknowledge the Hungarian government. We're Transylvanians. And before that, Rumanians."

"Oh," Jessie said contritely.

"It goes back a long way, and gets a little confused," said Feodor. "To make a long story short, we came here because there's no longer any place for our people in the old country."

"Well, I think you came to the right place," said Jessie. "Most everyone here had some good reason for leaving Europe."

"It's a good place to be," Feodor agreed fiercely. "A man has a chance, by God, and there's no one to stop him but himself!"

"Hah!" Zascha gave him a scornful laugh and downed his wine. Jessie noticed that most of it dribbled down his chin. "You are a young fool, Feodor." He leaned forward and focused awkwardly on Jessie. "It is no different here, boy. There are nobles like her, and peasants like us. Who do you think gets the land in the end?"

"Zascha!" Gustolf jolted the table with his fist and went livid. He jerked out of his seat and faced the man in a rage. "This *noble,* as you call her, is a Starbuck. And who do you think pays your way from New York and helps you buy the land you sit on, eh? By God, you insult the guest who fills that fat belly of yours!"

"For her own profit, you can be sure!" roared Zascha. "There is always a reason someone gives you something, Gustolf. So they can someday steal it back, yes?"

Feodor came out of his chair, but Gustolf's big hand held him back. "No. It is my house, and I take care of it. Leave, Zascha. Now. You shame me at my table. You shame us all."

Zascha muttered to himself, but the look in Gustolf's eye brought him quickly to his feet. He lurched away from the table and slammed the heavy door behind him.

"I offer my apology," Gustolf told Jessie. "He . . . has

40

no understanding. I am afraid many of my people do not."

"Is that why some of them are determined to sell their land?"

For a moment, Gustolf was taken back. "So. We are back to this again, are we not?"

"Yes, Gustolf," Jessica said evenly. "We are. As I said before, it's none of my business what you do, but I'd like to know *why*. The loans you have from the Green River Land Company are low-interest, with a long payoff. And you've got our ironclad promise to buy your wheat at a very good price."

"Yes," Gustolf said wearily, "this is all true."

"And yet some of your people are willing to give that up and sell out? At ridiculously low prices?"

"More than some of them, I'm afraid."

Jessie looked at him. "What do you mean?"

"I think you'd better go ahead and tell her," Feodor said softly.

Gustolf tried to face Jessie, but couldn't. "It is nearly all of us, Miss Jessica. The whole village wants to get out of Kansas and move west."

Jessie came suddenly alert. "You too?" She spread her hands in frustration. "But why? What is it, Gustolf? At least tell me that. Who's making these offers, and what are they telling you? They can't *make* you sell, you know!"

"No one is making us do anything," Gustolf said sharply. "We do what we—" He stopped suddenly. His blue-gray eyes went wide, and the blood drained from his face. "Hear it? Do you hear it?"

"Hear what?" asked Jessie.

Gustolf held up a trembling hand. Suddenly the sound came through the high window on the early night air—the far distant howl of a wolf.

"Oh, no!" Sonia gave a short little cry and brought her hand to her throat.

"It cannot be," Gustolf said harshly. "There is no full moon. It is not the right night!"

★

Chapter 5

"Gustolf, what on earth are you talking about?" asked Jessie. The old man stared right past her, jerked out of his chair, and bolted across the room to a door behind the big stove. Jessie exchanged a quick glance with Ki.

"Please. Stay where you are." Feodor leaned quickly across the table and gripped her arm. His dark eyes seemed to bore right through her. "Let him alone."

"What? Will someone *please* tell me what's going on here?"

Before Feodor could answer, Gustolf came out the back room and stomped to the front door. An old felt hat obscured his features, and he clutched a long wooden walking stick in his fist.

"Father, *no!*" Sonia gave a sharp little cry and threw herself in his arms. Gustolf shook her off without turning around. His face was dark and terrible. "Who else is to do this thing, eh? Who else?" His eyes swept to the younger man. "Feodor, see to the others. Do not come outside, Miss Starbuck. Stay here. You understand?"

"I'm damned if I will," said Jessie. "Look—"

"Wait, please!" Gustolf held up a hand and went rigid. Once more, the sonorous howl pierced the night. "Close," Gustolf said tightly. "It is much closer this time!" He opened the heavy door cautiously, sniffed the air, and then hurried across the empty common. Feodor moved after him, then turned back to Jessie and Ki.

"He's right, you know. It's best to stay here."

"Where is he going?" asked Ki. "It's the wolf, right?"

A shadow crossed Feodor's face. "Yes. It is the wolf."

"Then he'll need some help," said Jessie. "We'll be glad to do what we can."

"No." Feodor shook his head firmly. "Keep out of it. Please." He turned away and sprinted into the dark. Jessie gave Ki a look and started off across the common toward where Gustolf had disappeared. Ki caught up with her fast. Sonia cried out behind him, but neither Ki nor Jessie looked back.

"I'm not sure what's happening here," he told Jessie. "These people are acting most peculiar."

"I'll say they are." There was still a touch of purple in the sky, enough to make out the sod-roofed houses on either side and the open fields beyond. "That way, I think," said Jessie. "Ki, I can't figure this at all. There's not a soul out there but us and the old man. They're all locked up in those houses."

"Except Feodor. I think he's out here somewhere too."

"Wonderful," scoffed Jessie. "So where are the rest of the men? Looks to me like—"

Jessie froze. A ragged, unearthly scream shattered the night. "Lord God, what was that!"

"Not a wolf," Ki said sharply. "There—that way!" He pointed to the south, where the dark clump of trees lined the creek. Jessie sprinted after him, ankle-high grass brushing her boots. The land sloped down gradually from the settlement, then flattened again. A figure stood against the dark trees, just above the creek. Ki held up a hand and Jessie stopped.

"Gustolf?" Ki took a step forward.

"I am too late," Gustolf said dully. "He has struck already." The old man didn't turn. His gaze was fixed on the patch of ground before him. Ki moved up and looked. Jessie took a step and peered around him.

"Oh, no!" Her stomach drew up in a knot and she brought a hand to her breast. The day was fading quickly into night, but there was more than enough light to see the grisly thing sprawled in the grass at Gustolf's feet. It was a man, or what was left of him. He lay on his back, his mouth still open in a terrible, silent scream, eyes staring up at the dark. His throat had been completely ripped away, and the ground around him was black with his own blood. Jessie pulled her gaze from the sight. Whatever had attacked the man had been fast, and incredibly strong.

"It is young Michael Antonescu," Gustolf said soberly. "I will have to tell his wife. They have a child who is my godson." He bent to close the man's eyes, and for the first time seemed to notice that Jessie was there. "This is not a thing for a woman to see."

"I don't guess it's a thing for anyone to see," said Jessie. "I've seen some things about as bad as this, Gustolf. And I'm sorry about your friend." Jessie saw a match flare and turned to see Ki squatting down a few yards past the body. She walked to him quickly and peered over his shoulder at the tracks he was examining. A low whistle escaped her lips. "Now *that's* a big wolf. Good God, Ki!"

"It went up past the creek," said Ki. "Toward the wheatfields, I imagine."

"Gustolf," Jessie said, "if you can get some men together pretty quick, we might still track him. How many rifles do you have in the village?"

Gustolf pulled himself erect and stared. "You do not understand, do you? Guns are no good against the thing out there. It is not an ordinary wolf that did this to Michael Antonescu. It is a man-wolf, a werewolf."

"A *what!*" Jessica shrank back from the old man. "Gus-

45

tolf, you can't believe that. Werewolves are . . . just something in stories!"

"Stories, is it?" Gustolf looked woodenly at the mangled body at his feet. "I will tell this to the boy's wife and their son. I will tell them the American lady says their Michael was killed by something in a story."

"Please," sighed Jessie, "I'm sorry the man is dead." She moved around until she was between Gustolf and the body. "Look. The thing that killed Michael is just as real as you are."

"Oh, yes. It is real. I believe that."

"I do not think we are going to solve anything by talking out here," Ki said quietly.

"There is nothing to talk about," Gustolf said darkly. "Talking does not bring back the dead, and words will not stop the thing that is out there." He shook the black walking stick in his fist. "This! This is the only thing that soulless creature understands!"

"A cane?" Ki peered curiously at the thing. The handle was curved to fit the hand, and seemed to be made of some brightly polished metal. "I think I have read of this. The head is silver, is it not?"

"Of course it is." Gustolf gave him a withering look. "What else would it be but silver?"

"Is that supposed to mean something?" asked Jessie.

"Silver is purity. The werewolf is an impure thing."

"And?"

"And only silver can stop it, Miss Jessica. A blade, a bullet molded of the finest pure metal."

"And you believe that? Gustolf, I don't mean any disrespect—"

"I *don't* think it is a good idea to stand out here," Ki repeated firmly. He grabbed Jessie's arm. "If we are to talk, we can talk inside. There is nothing more to be done."

Ki turned as a voice called down from atop the hill and a bright torch flickered over the path. Feodor called again

46

and ran toward them, the dark-haired girl close on his heels.

"Sonia!" Gustolf went rigid and moved quickly to block his daughter's path.

"Father, you are all right?" She saw his face and looked puzzled. "What—what's back there? There's something, isn't there?"

"Nothing you need to see," he told her tightly. Gripping the girl's shoulders, he shot a furious glance at Feodor. "You bring her out here in the dark? Are you out of your mind?"

Feodor stood his ground. "I didn't bring her. She brought herself." He glanced past the old man's shoulder. "Who is it, Gustolf?"

"Michael. Michael Antonescu."

"Oh, *God!*" Sonia buried her face in her father's shoulder. Feodor touched her gently. "I will get her back to the house."

"An excellent idea," Gustolf said acidly. "One you should have thought of in the first place."

"It is not his fault," Sonia told him through her sobs. "It was my idea and—"

"I am not interested," sniffed Gustolf. "Get back now, and bar the door behind you this time."

Sonia looked up, startled. "You're not staying out here!"

"Of course I am," Gustolf said calmly. "I am the elder." He clutched the silver-headed cane. "The creature is still out there. It is my duty, and no other's."

"Then I am coming with you," Feodor said bluntly.

"You are taking Sonia back," Gustolf told him. "Do not cross me, boy!"

"There is nothing that says you have to go alone, Gustolf."

"Yes. There is. *I* say so."

Ki looked at Jessie, then turned to the old man. "You have no way of knowing whether the wolf is still out there. It might be best to try and pick up the trail in the morning."

47

"In the morning?" Gustolf looked at Ki as if he were a child. "In the *morning,* this creature will not be a wolf. He will be a man again."

"Yes, of course," Ki said evenly. "I forgot." He took a deep breath and turned back to Jessie. "I've got a pistol in my saddlebag at the house. Even if it won't harm this . . . werewolf, I would feel more comfortable to have it."

Gustolf scowled. "I did not ask you to come along. I do not need you or want you. You will be useless, and you'll get yourself killed!"

"I think it's a good idea," said Jessie.

"Pah!" Gustolf gave them all a withering stare and stalked off in the dark toward the wheatfields. "You do not understand. You know nothing of this!"

Jessie raised a thoughtful brow at Ki. "Be careful. All right?"

"You have no idea how careful I will be," Ki said soberly.

He stood perfectly still, letting his breath come in slow, even measures, feeling the tension flow out of his body. One part of his mind told him his old master, Hirata, would be proud of him; it is not an easy thing to achieve a state of calm when one is stalking a beast that has just tasted blood. The other, more Western side of his mind said he was an idiot. Following the old man into the fields was one of the dumbest things he'd ever done in his life. Ki was greatly inclined to agree with the latter. A samurai was supposed to have courage—but the other side of that coin was the wisdom to know when and how to use the arts at his disposal.

Now, he had already decided, was not one of those times. Gustolf was wandering about somewhere to his left. The stubborn old man had refused to let Ki anywhere near him. He was stomping around out there alone, confident in his belief that the silver-headed cane would protect him from evil. Ki couldn't share the man's faith. At the moment, he didn't feel protected at all. He felt naked, alone, and quite vulnerable. He had brought all of his samurai training to bear, but at the moment that training seemed next to useless. Being alert to sound and movement was no help at all. There was sound and movement all around him. A light breeze swept down the valley and whispered through the wheat. A million stalks and leaves rattled and brushed against their brothers. The field rippled and swayed like the waves of the sea. To Ki, though, it looked more like the bristling fur on the back of some ponderous beast...

He quickly swept the image aside, and brought all his senses to bear. A trained samurai could reach into a clamor of sound and movement and gingerly pluck out the ones that concerned him, those that presented a danger or told him something he needed to know. Now, though, that very ability seemed to be working against him. There was too much sound, too much motion. He wished his prey were a man instead of a beast. If it were—

Suddenly it struck him, and Ki nearly laughed out loud in spite of his danger. The ghost of his old teacher seemed to wag an admonishing finger in his face. It was foolish to blame the animal for not being a man. The samurai adapted himself to his enemy, learned to think like that enemy, learned to fight him on his own terms, with his own weapons.

Instantly, Ki dropped to the ground, let his hands and knees feel the still-warm soil of the wheatfield. The sounds and smells were entirely different here. He was part of the wolf's world now. He was a beast on four legs in a dark forest of slender and brittle trees.

He knelt in silence for a long moment, moved cautiously ahead, then stopped again to listen and sniff the air. There was the smell of the earth, and the dry, musty odor of wheat. And, gradually playing upon his senses, something else...

Ki came suddenly alert. The smell was stronger now— dark, musky, and alien. He moved again, then stopped and listened. It was still there. The thing was close. Too close!

49

He went to his belly and swept his eyes in a wide half-circle, straining to find his enemy in the dark. He could sense it, but couldn't pin it down. It was fast, as elusive as smoke—ahead of him now, moving steadily to the left. He could almost hear it, padding swiftly through the thick rows of wheat, not twenty yards away.

Faster, then faster still. It had abandoned all efforts at caution, and with a sudden chill, Ki understood why. *It no longer needed to stalk its prey . . . it knew exactly where it was!*

And in that instant, Ki knew the creature's path was all wrong—he had assumed the thing was stalking *him,* and this was not true at all . . .

"Gustolf—look out!" Ki sprang to his feet, and saw the old man far off to the left—fifty, sixty yards away. Gustolf saw the beast too, and froze in his tracks. The creature was a quick gray blur, bounding straight for him like the wind. The high wheat parted and went flat in its path. Ki set his legs, stretched the Colt in both hands. He squeezed off three quick shots, then broke into a run, knowing he'd never get there in time. The wolf would take Gustolf, tear out his throat as if he were a man made of straw . . .

The beast leaped, came clear out of the field with a snarl in its throat. Ki fired again and knew he'd missed. Gustolf screamed and went down. Ki jumped into the flattened clearing, pistol at the ready. The wolf saw him, raised its dark muzzle from Gustolf's chest, bared its teeth, and sprang straight for him. Ki jerked his body aside. Terrible jaws snapped at the air past his shoulder, and Ki felt the thing's breath on his cheek . . .

Then the creature was gone—only a crushed tangle of wheat showed where it had disappeared into the night. Ki came to his feet, crouching above Gustolf. He listened a moment, then turned quickly to the old man. His clothes were shredded, and his chest and arms were slick with blood. It was too dark to tell how badly he was hurt, and

Ki had no intention of inspecting the wounds there in the middle of the field.

When he lifted Gustolf in his arms, the old man groaned, opened his eyes wide, and stared up at Ki. "You...see, I told you. The bullets do not work...the thing cannot be killed that way...it is...no ordinary animal!"

"Don't talk," said Ki. "We will discuss the business of wolves at a later time."

"It is...true," Gustolf went on. "You can see that, can't you?"

"Old man, shut up!" Ki said sharply. "What I can *see* is that we are not yet out of this field. That thing is still out there, and at the moment it does not greatly matter what it might be. All right?"

Gustolf's eyes went dim, and he relaxed in Ki's arms. Ki quickened his steps, ignoring the man's considerable weight. He could feel the thing behind him, and didn't give a damn whether it was Oriental senses or Western imagination at work. All he wanted now was to put that dark sea of wheat at his back, and shut a stout wooden door behind him.

"Aaaaaaah!" Gustolf came suddenly awake. His eyes went wide and he clutched frantically at Ki, nearly spilling him to the ground. "Stop," he yelled hoarsely, "you must go back. Now!"

"Damn it," snapped Ki, "leave me alone, old man. I am doing the best I can!"

"No!" Gustolf shook his head wildly. "You...don't understand! The cane. It...it is still out there. I *must* have it. Without that...we are lost, all of us!"

Ki's arms were like lead. Gustolf pounded at him and kicked the air and cursed him in a tongue that seemed perfectly designed for that purpose. Ki walked stolidly on, praying he would reach the dark cottages before the wolf turned about and came at him, or the old man beat him to a pulp...

51

★

Chapter 6

Ki couldn't remember when a fire had seemed brighter, cheerier, more welcome. Jessie brought him coffee and he held the cup between his hands, enjoying the solid feel of the mug and the strong aroma of the dark and heady brew.

He understood what was happening. The fire, the mug, and the coffee were real and solid things, everyday objects from the world he lived in. They had nothing to do with shadow and superstition. His encounter with the wolf had shocked him more than a little. Nothing in his stern samurai training had prepared him for the thoughts that had preyed on his mind. He was more vulnerable to such things than he'd imagined.

Jessie sat down beside him and sipped her coffee. "He's going to be all right," she said. "Scratched up pretty badly and he lost some blood, but you got to him in time." She nodded over her shoulder at the back room. "Sonia brought in an old lady who has to be a hundred and ten. Did you see her? She's got bags of leaf mold and little clay pots of stuff that smells bad. Nothing you ever saw in a doctor's office, but it seems to do the job. You're not listening to me at all, are you?"

Ki looked up quickly. "Yes. And no, Jessie. I'm afraid I'm only partly here at the moment."

"That business out there got to you, didn't it?"

"Yes, it did. Very much."

She studied him thoughtfully. "I don't see any reason why it shouldn't, Ki. You don't have to believe in all this for it to affect you. Wolfsbane and silver bullets and things howling outside..." She hugged her shoulders and shivered. "Gives *me* the creeps, I'll tell you."

Ki nodded in agreement. "Fear and superstition are most infectious diseases. My problem is, I didn't think I could catch it."

"Ki..."

He shrugged and shot her a weary grin. "Don't worry. I am half Japanese and half American. As far as I know, there are no Transylvanians on either side of my family." His smile faded and he stared into the fire. "I see, though, what has happened to these people. And I understand *how* it could happen. I think you do too."

"Oh, yes. I do, Ki." She sipped her coffee and set it down.

"This is a strange business, Jessie. I don't know what to make of it. There were no stock out there by the creek, you know. The few animals they have are all penned up right here in the village."

"Wolves have been known to attack people before," Jessie reminded him.

"Yes, they have. But not without some reason. If they are starving, for instance. Or cornered, with no way out. Neither of those things happened here."

"No, so what's the answer?"

Ki shrugged. "I don't know, but—" He stopped abruptly and turned, peering about the room. "Jessie, where is Feodor? I just remembered I haven't seen him since I brought in Gustolf."

Jessie winced. "I forgot to tell you. He went out *there*, Ki."

54

"In the fields?" Ki shook his head in wonder. "Is everyone crazy around here? I don't suppose he's armed, or that anyone went with him?"

Before Jessie could answer, Sonia came in from the back room, slumped wearily against the table, and ran a hand through her hair.

"There's still some coffee," said Jessie. She got up and laid a hand on the girl's shoulder. "Why don't you sit down and get some rest? Your father's going to be just fine, Sonia. He's a strong man, and he'll heal fast. In a few days—"

Sonia jerked away, dark eyes blazing with anger. "My father was right. You understand nothing, do you? He will not be 'just fine,' Miss Starbuck!"

"But he will, Sonia—"

"No!" Tears streaked her cheeks. "Do you know what our people are doing now? They are gathered in one of the cottages. They pray to the saints that Gustolf dies, that his wounds will not heal. That is my prayer as well!"

"What?" Jessie caught the girl and turned her roughly around. "Sonia—you can't mean that!"

A low cry caught in the girl's throat and she sank to a chair and buried her face in her hands. "If—if a werewolf brings blood to a human, the blood of the creature itself taints its victim." She peered up at Jessie, her features strained with fear. "If my father should live, then he will become as the man-wolf himself, at the next full moon!"

Jessie moved toward her. "No!" The girl shrank away. "You don't understand. You don't know about these things."

"I know that you're terribly frightened. That you *believe* that's what will happen. But it won't, Sonia, really."

Sonia laughed through her tears. "You would know this, of course. A rich lady from America has great knowledge of my country and what happens there."

"I don't know Transylvania, or anything about you and your people," Jessie admitted. "I *do* know men don't turn into wolves."

55

"You know nothing!" snapped Sonia.

"Please." Ki stood and faced the girl. "Can you tell me what Feodor is doing in the fields? Why did he go there?"

Sonia's face fell. "He had to. There was no one else."

"No one else to do what?"

"To get the cane, of course!"

Ki sighed and let out a breath. "Yes. The cane. Your father was raving about that when I carried him back."

Sonia turned her anger on Ki. "He was not *raving* at all. He knew he had lost the cane, and that it had to be retrieved. Even at the price of his life—even if he had *not* been bitten by the thing. You should have let him do as he wished."

"It did not seem like a sound idea at the moment."

"Because you have no understanding," scoffed Sonia. "Why do you think Feodor is risking his life now to try to find it? My father is the Keeper of the Silver Cane. The cane is our life, our only protection. It has been passed from elder to elder for hundreds of years, from one generation to the next. It is all we have to face the powers of the devil's creatures on Earth!" Sonia moaned and tore at her face. "God, why am I telling you this?" You don't believe a word of it."

"We believe you and your people are very troubled by this thing," Ki said gently.

"Troubled! Is that what you think is happening here? Trouble?" The girl stood, straightened her skirts, and walked unsteadily to the big stove. "I cannot understand what happened," she said, almost to herself. "Things are not the same in America." She turned and looked at Jessie. "That is why my father let you stay for supper. He thought it was safe for you to ride out of here after dark. In our country, a man cannot become a wolf unless the moon is full. That would not happen for another three days. Yet the creature has killed. Why? Why has this—" Sonia's face twisted in fury and grief, and she fled from the room and closed the door behind her.

Jessie rolled her eyes at Ki, filled her mug again, then

changed her mind and set it aside. "Lord, Ki, I don't think you could convince these folks if you skinned that wolf and nailed its hide to the wall."

"A belief is harder to kill than a whole pack of wolves. It will take more than that." He moved toward the door and turned to face her. "I'm going to take a look around. I'll be right back."

Jessie nearly came out of her chair. "Ki, you are not thinking about going after Feodor?"

"No. That occurred to me, but only briefly." Ki grinned and shook his head. "The Japanese have a saying: 'Do not rescue a Transylvanian from the wheatfields. He will likely never forgive you.'"

Jessie smiled thinly at him.

The women of the village might be praying their elder would die, but Ki found the men engaged in other pursuits. They were huddled on the edge of the common, squatting against the wall of a cottage. A convenient open doorway was nearby. A bottle of wine was making the rounds, and several of the men puffed big curved pipes full of black and pungent tobacco.

Ki didn't mean to stop in the shadows. He would have walked past the group and kept going if a familiar voice hadn't caught his attention. It was Zascha, their unpleasant supper companion of a few hours before. Ki had no idea what he was saying, but the man's tone was unmistakable. He was stomping up and down before his friends, flailing his arms about and spitting out his anger.

He's stirring them up about something, thought Ki, and doing a pretty fair job of it. As he watched, Zascha gestured toward the fields, then back to Gustolf's cottage. Twice, Ki picked Jessie's name out of the unfamiliar tongue. Each time Zascha mentioned her, his listeners muttered darkly to themselves, slammed their fists together, and gravely shook their heads.

Ki walked quietly away, circled the cottages, and looked

out into the night. Every town had at least one troublemaker, and the sour-faced Zascha clearly had the job sewn up in Gustolf's village. Ki would have given much to know what the man was saying, but figured he had a fair idea already. The American girl was not to be trusted. She had come to lure the elder into her web, to fleece the village before they could sell their land and move on. And look what had happened—on the very night she and the Oriental had arrived. One of their own had been killed, and old Gustolf himself was doomed, bitten by the man-wolf. Did the villagers need any more proof that the place called Kansas was not for them?

Maybe it wasn't exactly like that, thought Ki—but it was likely close enough. Zascha would do his damnedest to—

A boot scraped earth behind him and Ki threw himself aside, feeling the weapon slice air only inches from his shoulder. He rolled, and came up on his haunches in a crouch. The man came at him like a bull, whipping the club before him in a quick, vicious arc. Ki stepped deftly away, heard the other man too late, and took the big fist on his shoulder. Ki staggered, stumbling away from his attackers. The first man yelled and came at him, raised the club, and swept it at Ki's head. Ki twisted and found his footing, caught the weapon in his fist, and swung the man aside.

His other assailant was more cautious now. He circled Ki warily, waiting for his friend. Ki watched him. They wanted to get him between them—one in front and the other in back. He moved in close to the man he could see and let them have their way. The man backed off, drawing Ki toward him. Ki sensed the other man, felt him right behind him.

Suddenly he feinted toward the man in front, twisted, and moved in a blur. His foot lashed out and caught the man behind him in the gut. The man cried out, dropped his weapon, and clutched his belly. Ki kicked him solidly in the throat, hard enough to down him without snapping his neck.

When he turned, the other man was coming at him. Ki stood his ground. The man stopped, surprised to see his foe simply standing there waiting for the blow. Then the tendons tightened in his arms and he swept the air with his club, forcing Ki back. He'd learned a few lessons and was taking his time. Now he held the club in a shorter, easier grip, with both hands, grasping the weapon close to the chest and making it hard for Ki to come at him.

Ki watched the man's eyes, the muscles in his neck. The man swung, again and again. Each time, Ki took a step back, knowing the instant before the blow was coming. The man tried to throw him off, feinting, then coming in fast. Ki waited. The man came at him again and Ki ducked, digging his heels in the earth and launching himself like a spring at the man's legs.

The attacker shouted and flailed his arms. The club fell away. Ki slammed him hard against the ground. The man rolled, swung a big fist, and caught Ki's jaw. Ki spit blood and wiped his mouth. The man scrambled to his feet. Ki hit him—short, punishing blows that whipped inside the man's guard. The man swung wildly at Ki, but Ki merely jerked his head aside and let the blows pass. He came inside the man's arms and slapped him with three rapid blows across the face. The man staggered. His arms went limp and a glaze covered his eyes. Ki tapped him lightly on the jaw and turned away, not even waiting to watch him fall.

As he turned, Ki saw something move in the shadow of one of the cottages. He couldn't see who it was, but it didn't take much to guess.

"Zascha," he said softly, "you send other men to do your work. You should come and try yourself." The shadow didn't answer. When Ki looked again, it was gone.

Jessie turned as Feodor opened the door to the night and closed it quickly behind him. "Well, I'm glad you're back safe," she said. "Is anything out there?"

"If it is, I didn't see it," he said flatly. "And that is fine with me." He looked at Jessie, then past her to the closed door of Gustolf's room. "I found it," he said, holding up the cane for her to see. "The old man will be relieved. How is he? Was he badly hurt?"

"No, he's all right. Sonia's with him now. I think she probably passed out from exhaustion." Jessie turned her head slightly and watched Feodor as he slipped off his jacket and heated the last of the coffee on the stove. He was a strange man, and she wasn't yet sure what to make of him. He was darkly attractive, and she liked the way he handled himself—calm and self-assured, saying what he felt like saying and keeping the rest to himself. More than once during supper she'd caught his eyes on her, and Jessie knew exactly what he was thinking. He was wondering how it would be to go to bed with her, and had already decided it was a fine idea. Jessie had to admit the same thought had crossed her mind. She was honest in her feelings toward a man, and her instincts seldom betrayed her. She had a good feeling about this one, but there was . . . *something* that wasn't quite right. She decided it had a lot to do with what was happening here, and how much of it Feodor did and didn't believe.

He turned suddenly, and caught her watching him. He gave her a broad grin, and Jessie didn't turn away. "What are you thinking?" he asked.

"You sure you want to hear?"

"Yes. I am certain I do."

"I was thinking," Jessie said, "that going back out there after that cane was either a very brave or a very foolhardy thing to do."

Feodor closed one eye, the coffee cup halfway to his mouth. "I would think I am closer to a fool than a hero. If you want to know the truth, I was guided more by guilt than anything else." A shadow crossed his face. "I should not have let him go out there alone. That was wrong."

"Why? Because of the wolf—or the man-wolf?"

Feodor's mouth tightened into a firm and thoughtful line. "You ask an honest question. I will give you the best answer

60

I can. I went to the university in Vienna. It was very hard for my family to send me there. I tried to become an attorney. Yet I am not an attorney. I am a farmer. See?" He smiled slightly and held out his open palms.

Jessie reached out and touched them, felt the callused texture of his skin, and the strength in the tendons beneath. "Not a lawyer's hands, that's for sure."

Feodor shrugged. "I have answered your question, yes? I am caught between the new and the old. I do not believe in werewolves, Jessica Starbuck, but I understand the fears of my people. They have a new land now, but it is hard for them to let go of the one they left behind."

"May I see that thing?" asked Jessica. She nodded toward the cane, and Feodor handed it to her.

"Sort of—beautiful and awful at the same time, isn't it?"

"Yes. I would say that is so."

The can was not painted black, as she had first supposed. It was simply darkened and stained with age. It was the silver head, though, that intrigued her. It was fashioned roughly in the shape of an **L**—part of the angle made to fit the hand, the other part curved to clamp tightly over the cane. The silver head formed the muzzle, eyes and long ears of a wolf. The lower angle curled down over the cane in the thick fur of the creature's neck and shoulders. Jessie pressed her hand tightly around the head, then jerked it quickly away.

"It's—cold," she said, widening her eyes in surprise. "Why would it be that cold?"

"I suppose because it is silver," he said. A slight smile touched the corner of his mouth, and Jessie caught it.

"All right," she said wearily, "let's not get dark and mysterious."

"I didn't say a thing," Feodor said blandly.

"Good. Just don't. Feodor, that is a real wolf out there. Ki says he's nearly certain he hit it at least once. He's a good shot, too."

"Good shots miss."

"I know they do. Maybe Ki *did* miss. Or maybe he didn't. Maybe the wolf went off and died somewhere."

Feodor gave her a look. "No one in this village is going to believe that, Jessica."

"No, I don't suppose they will." Jessica paused a moment. "Feodor, how long has the settlement been here?"

"A year and a half. No, closer to two."

"And when did you start having...wolf trouble?"

"Two months ago. A young girl was attacked and killed. Only eight years old."

"What?" Jessie sat up straight. "I didn't know about that."

Feodor let out a breath, searched through his pockets, and began thumbing tobacco into a heavy briar pipe. "She was bringing up stock. Down by the creek, just after sundown. We—many of us—heard her scream. The thing nearly tore her in half...dragged her a good hundred yards before he...left her alone."

Jessie read the hard lines of pain in his face. "And you hadn't seen any wolves before that? Not any?"

"Never." He looked squarely at Jessie. "The girl was killed under a full moon. You can imagine what my people thought of that."

"But it's not a full moon now, is it? Sonia said it won't be for another three days. How do they explain that?"

"Explain?" Feodor's calm features suddenly exploded in anger. "My God, a man is dead, and you talk of explanations! I—" He let out a breath and ran a hand through his hair. "Forgive me. I had no cause for that."

"Forget it. Maybe I was asking too many questions."

"I would not be much of a lawyer," Feodor said, smiling, "if I can be injured by a few questions. The learned masters at the university were tyrants. We were taught to ask questions—*and* answer them—in our sleep."

"Do you think you'll ever go back to that?"

"I don't know." He looked down at his hands. "What

I told you a moment ago was the truth, Jessica. I am not yet sure which Feodor I really am."

"Well, anyway," she said gently, "whichever you turn out to be, I know you'll be the best."

Feodor caught the tone of her voice. He looked up quickly, and his dark eyes flashed a message Jessie had no trouble at all understanding. She met his gaze boldly and returned it.

Feodor started to speak, then thought better of it. He started for the door and stopped to face her. "You and Ki will stay here in the village tonight, of course. I'll arrange for it with some of our people."

"Thank you. I appreciate that."

"Well, then . . ." Feodor looked at her. "Well, good night, Jessica." He turned quickly and left the cottage.

Jessie wasn't sure what woke her.

She sat up straight and cocked her head to listen. When her eyes got used to the dark, she slipped out of bed and walked quietly across the unfamiliar room to the window. The near-full moon was hidden behind pale, fast-moving clouds. Jessie could just make out the dim shapes of the cottages nearby, and the dark, flat horizon farther away.

Maybe it was nothing at all, she decided. Part of a dream that had brought her up out of sleep. *That* would certainly be no surprise, she told herself wearily. After the day's bizarre events, sleep hadn't come easily at all, and when it did—

Jessie's heart leaped up in her throat. She pressed her hands against the sill and peered out into the night. There was something . . . something . . .

Suddenly the low clouds scudded aside and the moon flooded the earth with cold white light. The thing was a good twenty yards from Jessie's window, just past the last cabin in the village. At first it was no more than the night itself, another part of the dark. Then, as the clouds rushed by, it seemed to draw strength and body from the moon,

63

changing before her eyes from shadow to wispy gray. It stood there a long moment, silent and unmoving. Then, sweeping its head around, it turned and walked away into the fields.

Jessie reached blindly for a straight-back chair and eased herself down. She tried to keep from shaking, but couldn't. It was easy to tell herself the thing she'd seen wasn't there—that it was a trick of the light and her own imagination. She knew, though, that wasn't so.

★

Chapter 7

Jessie hadn't been asleep again for more than an hour when the settlement began to stir. Like any farming community, the day's work began before sunrise. A milk cow bawled, and chickens began clucking about outside the window. Cookpans rattled on the stove, and one enterprising farmer started nailing a broken fence when there was scarcely light to see it.

Jessie moaned and gave up, stumbled out of bed, and searched out her clothes in the half dark. The family who'd put her up invited her to breakfast in broken English, and Jessie accepted.

She found Ki waiting across the common, and strolled down to meet him. Like Jessie, he was wearing the same clothes he'd put on the day before, since neither had anticipated spending the night outside of Roster. His well-worn denims were faded nearly white, and the loose-fitting cotton twill shirt had been washed so often it had no color at all. A battered Stetson and an old leather jacket completed his outfit. She saw he had thrust a pair of the wicked, two-pronged *sai* under his belt, weapons he could use in a dozen different ways.

"I will not ask if you rested well," said Ki. "I'm sure

you slept no better than I did."

"Good," Jessie said dully. "I'm glad you're not asking. Because I certainly don't care to talk about it. Three hours in two nights just isn't very satisfying." She looked past Ki to the sod-roofed cottage at the end of the common. "Have you seen anyone yet? I was wondering how the old man is doing."

"I saw him," said Ki. "Physically, he is doing well. The wounds are not infected. It is his mind that has been poisoned, Jessie. He's convinced the creature's blood now flows in his veins. That he will become a man-wolf when the moon is full. I cannot—" Ki stopped and gave her a puzzled frown. "Jessie, what's wrong?"

"Uh, nothing, I guess." Jessie shrugged, but Ki's eyes wouldn't leave her. She shot him a weak little grin. "Can't keep any secrets from you, can I? Ki, something happened last night. I'm not at all sure what. I saw something. Out there, in the middle of the night." She told him, then, about waking and watching the spectral shape appear in the moonlight, then move off into the darkness. She told it exactly as she'd seen it, leaving nothing out.

Ki put a hand to his face and studied her thoughtfully. "No wonder you didn't get any sleep."

"It's crazy, isn't it? Ki, I could have seen something and let my imagaination take it from there, I guess, but—"

"But you didn't, did you?"

"No. I didn't. It was there. I did see something." She bit her lip nervously. "What do you figure it was? I mean, besides a werewolf? I don't care *what* it looked like, I am not ready for that."

"I'm not either. And that tells us something, doesn't it? You either saw a real werewolf, or something that looked like one. If we cannot accept the first, that leaves us with an interesting question. What looks like a man-wolf and isn't?"

"Someone who *wants* to look like one?"

Ki nodded. "A most intriguing possibility."

Jessie took a few steps, toeing her boots into the ground. "I don't know," she said hesitantly. "Whatever that thing was doing out there, it wasn't for my benefit. It didn't know I was going to be watching."

"No," Ki agreed, "it had some other purpose for prowling around the village."

Jessie let her eyes sweep the horizon, past the dark fields of wheat to the somber line of trees by the creek. The sky was pale blue in the east, but the sod-roofed cottages and the people moving about were still gray and indistinct. "All right." Jessie let out a breath. "Wolves and other spooks aren't all we've got to worry about, Ki. I'm determined to find out who's after these folks' land, and I think the answer's out here. We won't learn much back in Roster."

Ki thought a minute. "While you're pursuing that, maybe I can learn something about things that prowl around in the night."

"Oh?" Jessie gave him a skeptical frown. "How do you figure on doing this?"

"By using mysterious Oriental methods," Ki grinned. "Lying a little, looking in the wrong direction, and appearing to do something else entirely."

Jessie made a noise in her throat. "Nothing real Oriental about that, friend. Sounds to me like a couple of St. Louis bankers making a deal."

The funeral of Michael Antonescu took place on a barren hilltop just east of the settlement. It was nearly ten in the morning, and Ki was already gone. Jessie stood apart, watching two of the young man's broad-shouldered relatives carry the greenwood coffin slowly past the common and up the hill. Gustolf led the widow carrying her son, and the rest of the villagers followed. Jessie fell in behind, keeping the respectful distance of an outsider. The ceremony was short. In less than half an hour, the settlers were back at work under the broiling summer sun. Except for the fresh dirt of a new grave, it was hard to tell that anything unusual had happened.

Jessie knew she ought to be asking questions, but decided this particular morning wasn't the right time for it. She had no desire to talk to Gustolf, and a quick look from Sonia at the funeral did nothing to change her mind. Instead, she found her Colt in her saddlebag and stuck it out of sight under her jacket, then wandered out of the settlement to the dark line of trees that masked the creek.

The creek seemed a world away from the hot plains of Kansas. The waterway had clearly been there a long time, for the years had cut through hard stone banks a good ten feet down to the creek itself. Jessie was surprised to find nearly three feet of water coursing by in places. In this part of the country in midsummer, it could easily have been bone dry.

She wandered through the trees for nearly a mile, enjoying the walk and keeping one eye open for sign. At first she felt uneasy, going so far from the settlement. The young man *had* been killed near the creek, and so had the girl. Ki wouldn't approve, Jessie knew—but it was broad daylight, and even in the thicket of trees she could see a good distance around her. And if any wolves had passed this way, they'd left no tracks behind.

At noon she found a bend in the creek where the water had carved a clear, deep pool in comparatively soft rock. The bottom was covered in white gravel, and looked seven or eight feet deep. Jessie couldn't resist. It had been more than twenty-four hours since she'd stepped off the Kansas Pacific, in the same denims and shirt she was wearing now. It didn't seem likely any settlers would venture this far, even in daylight—not with the events of the night before fresh in their minds.

Making her way down the steep bank, she laid her jacket aside, perched on a flat rock, and eased off her boots and socks. Lowering her feet into the cool water was almost more than she could stand. Jessie closed her eyes and gave

68

a long sigh of pleasure. The feeling was almost sensuous. She knew exactly how it would feel when she slipped her whole body into the creek, and could hardly wait to get out of her clothes. Standing up to her ankles in the shallow end of the pool, she drew down the brown Stetson and ran long fingers through her strawberry-blonde mane, tossing it free and easy over her shoulders. She pulled the blouse out of her denims, quickly loosed the buttons, and slipped the silk garment off her shoulders. She laid the Colt within reach near the edge of the pool, laying the edge of her blouse over the barrel. The garter rig she usually wore around her thigh was loose in the pocket of her jacket, and she let that stay where it was. If anything large and furry disturbed her bath, she certainly didn't intend to face it with a derringer. Taking a last quick look at the creek bank above, she hopped about on one foot and peeled herself out of the tight denims.

Lord the water looked good! Jessie figured on giving her clothes a good soaking, then wearing them back in the sun to let them dry. That, however, was a chore—and a little lazy pleasure came first.

She stopped at the shallow bank and stretched luxuriantly, raising her arms high over her head and lifting herself on the balls of her feet. The motion flattened the slight swell of her belly and tauntened the gentle curves of her breasts. Jessie closed her eyes and let her naked body drink in the warm rays that dappled the pool through the trees. The pleasure of the water awaited her, and anticipating that pleasure, putting it off another moment—

A dead branch snapped like a shot on the bank overhead. Jessie's lean figure moved in a blur of white. In one fluid motion she turned on her heels, bent her legs in a crouch, twisted at the waist, and scooped up the revolver. Before the second heavy foot cut through the silence, the .38's muzzle was sweeping the bank in a steady arc.

A face suddenly appeared over Jessie's gunsights. Feodor stared down at her a brief moment before it dawned on him what he was seeing.

"J-Jessica!" Feodor looked appalled, turned red, and

gazed quickly up at the trees. "Please. You mustn't think I was, uh—"

"Sneaking up on me for a peek?" Jessie gave him a grin and lowered the pistol.

"Yes. No! I saw you leave the village. I followed you, but I never—"

"I know that," said Jessie. "Feodor, no one sneaking up on a girl would make *that* much noise—or look as surprised as you did. Quit searching up there for birds and come on down."

"Is it all right if I turn around? Are you—"

"Decent?" Jessie laughed, and put her hands on her hips. "Feodor," she said gently, "I haven't slipped into a corset and a long gown, if that's what you mean. I *guess* I look decent, though. As much as I did the last time you looked."

Feodor returned her laugh, then faced her and met her gaze squarely. "If I don't break my neck getting down, I'll be right there."

"Take your time," said Jessie. "I'm not going anywhere." She watched him scramble down the steep bank, sending a shower of loose stones rattling into the water. Before he reached the creekbed, she waded into the water up to her knees, then pushed off and swam to the middle of the pool.

Feodor walked up to the shallows and slapped rock dust off his knees. "How's the water?"

"Perfect," Jessie called back. "What's keeping you?"

Feodor nodded. Without a word, he sat down and pulled off his heavy work boots, then stood and jerked the worn pullover shirt over his shoulders and snaked out of his trousers. He smiled at Jessie, then walked into the water and moved toward her with long, even strokes. He'd taken his time undressing and coming to her, which seemed only fair to Jessie. He'd gotten a look at her, then given her time to do some admiring of her own. She liked what she saw— he was lean and hard-bodied, dark-skinned even where the sun hadn't touched him. A light matting of hair trailed in an inverted vee down his chest and past his belly. Jessie's

70

gaze rested a long moment between his legs. Feodor saw her, and she gave him back a bold, unashamed grin.

He paddled up to her and treaded water. "If I'm not mistaken, that was what you Americans call a leer, was it not?"

Jessie laughed and splashed him with water. "That's what it was, friend. I'll bet you have a word just like it in Rumanian, too."

"We have been known to leer now and then," he said solemnly. "This is true."

Jessie swam toward the edge of the pool until her feet touched bottom. Feodor joined her, reached out, and circled her waist with his hands.

Jessie put her hands on his shoulders and looked up at him. "I could lie to you, you know, and say I was shocked to find you up on that bank, and me standing down here stark naked."

"You weren't, though, were you?"

"No. To be honest, it felt very good, Feodor. Very good, very comfortable, and . . . exciting, at the same time. Being naked with you seems like the right thing to do. If it didn't, I certainly wouldn't be here." She laughed and kissed him lightly on the cheek. "Anyway, it's the second time you've seen me, you know. I couldn't feel any more naked now than I did last night. When you looked at me across the table." Jessie shuddered and bit her lip. "Mister, you were doing all *kinds* of things to me with your eyes."

Feodor looked up at the trees. "Jessica Starbuck, you cannot even imagine the things I was doing."

"Well. We'll see about that, I guess, won't we? I—oh, *my!*" Jessie felt his hands slide up from the curve of her waist to cup her breasts in his palms. His fingers caressed her gently, squeezing her just enough to bring the rosy tips out of the water. The sudden touch of the air brought out goosebumps, and tightened her nipples into hard nubbins of pink.

Jessie felt her pulse quicken under his touch. His hands

71

slid over her water-slick skin, leaving bright droplets that sparkled in the sun. His dark eyes never left her; his fingers moved lazily past the swell of her breasts, under her arms, and down the slender bow of her back to the curve of her hips. He stopped there, and rested his hands under her buttocks and brought her to him. Jessie felt the whole delicious length of him against her. She marveled at the softness of her breasts against the hard curve of his chest, the fierce, exciting press of his erection on her belly. She looked up at him and gave a joyous little laugh, reached out and teased a strand of hair off his brow.

"You know what I feel like?" she said.

"I know exactly what you feel like," he told her.

"No, that is *not* what I mean." She pressed a finger against his lips. "Don't laugh now. I feel like...like an otter."

Feodor laughed and held her tight.

"See? You did laugh," she scolded. "I always wondered why they looked as if they were enjoying themselves. Now I know why."

"Somehow, I don't think otters have this much fun."

"Sure they do. They just don't tell anyone. Mmmm, yes!" She curled her arms about his neck, then arched her back lazily away from him until her coppery hair nearly touched the water. The motion pressed her belly hard against him. Feodor's hands grasped the slender circle of her waist, pulled her gently to him, then released her and pulled her to him again. Jessie thrust herself against him, relaxed in his arms, and let his body and the buoyancy of the water take her where she wanted to go. The head of his member lightly stroked her belly, while the hard base of the shaft pressed the sensitive crown of her pleasure. Cool water flowed around her, lubricating the exquisitely gentle touch of his body. The growing warmth in her thighs coursed the length of her legs, raced up to her breasts, and finally radiated to every point in her body.

Feodor released her waist and let his hands find the swell

72

of her bottom. As if some silent signal had passed between them, Jessie let her legs swing free in the water. His hands in the small of her back kept her afloat as her thighs parted eagerly to take him in.

Jessie gave a soft purr of joy as he entered her. She reached up and wrapped her arms about his neck, resting her cheek against his chest. Her legs scissored his waist, and Feodor's hands clasped the firm mounds of her hips to draw her closer still. For a long moment she lay there against him, clinging to him, relishing the warmth of his presence inside her. Then she began to grind herself slowly against him, moving her softness in slow, lazy circles. Feodor stood still in the water, holding her body against him, letting her bring them both to pleasure. She threw back her head and looked at him, watched the tightness at the corners of his mouth, the dark intensity of his eyes. For a quick moment she slammed herself hard against him, as if she meant to end it there. Feodor sucked in breath and closed his eyes. Jessie laughed, slowed her pace abruptly, and let him slide nearly all the way out of her body. Feodor opened his eyes and grinned. She gave him a teasing wink, drew him slowly within her again, then out and in once more.

The agony and pleasure of her loving was ready to push him into a final explosion. Jessie could see it in his eyes. The sensitive edge of her own sweet release was a warm and exquisite glow between her thighs. The pain and anticipation she saw in his face heightened her joy, swept her along until she no longer cared to contain it. A small cry stuck in her throat and she thrust herself against him, opening her lips hungrily to let his tongue lovingly fill her mouth, as that other member swelled to fill her below . . .

★

Chapter 8

Jessie lay on her side, her head cradled in the hollow of his arm. Bright shafts of afternoon sun pierced the trees to dapple the sandy bank. She opened one eye and peered lazily down the length of his chest. Gold coins of light patterned his flesh and danced across the creamier tones of her leg. Jessie purred and snuggled closer, pressing her breasts against him and sliding her thigh across his belly. Feodor raised himself up on his arms, tumbled her easily onto her back, and found her mouth with his own.

"Well!" Jessie sucked in a breath and let it sigh through her lips. "That was certainly a fine kiss, mister."

"Good. It was supposed to be." He fingered a strawberry-colored curl on her cheek. "Your hair still has little drops of water here and there. They look like tiny diamonds."

Jessie leaned up and smiled. "I think I've been making love to a poet."

"All Transylvanians are poets," he told her. "Didn't you know that? We are surrounded by dark, gloomy mountains, thick forests, and deep rivers. A man either takes to drink in such a place or writes poems about it. Most of my people cannot afford that much to drink, so..."

Jessie laughed at that. "I think *some* of your people take time to become lovers, Feodor. I know one who did. And a very good lover, at that."

"Jessica...how could a man give you any less than everything he has?"

"Oh, I expect that's possible," she grinned.

He shook his head and let his eyes wander freely over her body. His look was so intense, she could almost feel it brushing her skin. He started at her legs, moved up the gentle curve of her thighs, and let his gaze rest lovingly on the soft nest of hair burnished copper in the sun. She felt him there, warming the fires inside—almost as if he'd reached between her legs again and touched her. She squirmed under his bold tour of her treasures, and arched her back off the ground like a cat. The motion made a satiny hollow in her belly, and thrust her breasts up to meet him. Feodor bent to stroke her tightened nipples with his tongue, pulling the sweet tips into his mouth.

"Yes," cried Jessie, "oh, *yes!*" With each silken touch she felt the warmth within her grow. It flowed like thick and sugary syrup from her thighs up to the hard points of her breasts. Feodor moved over her again, and she reached down eagerly to grasp the hardness she knew was waiting for her touch. Opening her legs wide, she guided him gently through the moist folds of her flesh, opening to him like a flower. He rested just inside her, filling her but hardly moving at all.

Jessie delighted in the slow, exquisite touch of his erection, and answered that touch with an easy pressure of her own. Feodor looked down and grasped her chin in his hands. "Jessica—may I say something to you?"

"Of course," she said softly. "You can say anything you like to me."

"I want you to take this...as I mean it. There are not many women like you. Not anywhere. Do you know this?"

"Just what kind of woman do you think I am, Feodor?"

"I think you are a woman who is honest in her feelings.

76

Who is not . . . ashamed to let herself be what she is. You show a man that you . . ." Feodor stopped to find the words. ". . . that you relish the pleasure of making love. Am I saying this right?"

"Oh, I think you're doing pretty well," she teased. "Relish, huh?" She bit her lip and gave him a saucy grin. "You mean like this, do you?" Very gently, she contracted her loins around him, stroking his erection until she could feel it begin to swell inside her.

"Ahhhh!" Feodor's eyes went wide. "Uh, yes. I think that's exactly what I mean. Jessica, you do that again and I'll—"

"Now that's not much of a threat, Feodor. At least not one that scares me." She reached up and touched a finger to his lips. "You filling me up again comes under the heading of relishing the pleasures of making love. When you did that to me in the pool . . ." She closed her eyes and grinned. "That was perfectly beautiful." She pulled him to her and kissed him. "You are a good man, Feodor. And yes, you're right. I don't see anything wrong with showing what I feel. If you can't, I think you're making love to the wrong person, and shouldn't be there in the first place. I could thank *you* for being what you are too, you know. I wanted you, just as you wanted me. We let each other know that. It would be sad if we hadn't, wouldn't it?"

"I don't think there was any danger of that, do you?" He leaned down and took her in his arms, and for a long moment he stroked her slowly, thrusting himself against her, then drawing out again. Jessie lay back on the warm sand and closed her eyes. Each new stroke brought her closer, then closer still . . .

"You like that, don't you?" he whispered. "Everything I do to you . . ."

"Yes. Oh, yes! God, Feodor, now. It's time now, isn't it?"

Once more she clasped her long legs lovingly about him, pressed herself against him, and ground her fingers into the hard muscle of his shoulders. They were poised and ready, both of them, balancing on the thin edge of their pleasure— a breath, a whisper, a soft touch away from the thing they would bring to each other. Feodor thrust himself against her, burying himself in the warmth of her flesh. Jessie arched her belly up joyously to meet him, drawing him hungrily to her. Her hands left his shoulders and slid along the curve of his back to grasp his hips. When he plunged into her again, she dug her nails sharply into his skin.

Feodor shuddered and bellowed out his pleasure. Jessie closed her eyes, clinging to him as if his body were somehow hers as well, as if the fire that exploded between them fused them together. Feodor cried out again, and once more she felt him rush into her like a flood. His pleasure heightened her own, reached down and stirred the warmth within her. This time her orgasm was nearly an agony of delight, a force that lifted her up and swept her along in its fury. For a while she was almost certain it would never end—half afraid that it would, half afraid that it wouldn't...

Finally, Feodor let out a breath, rolled over on his back, and drew Jessie over onto his chest. "I think you are right," he said solemnly. "There is much to be said for pleasure between a man and a woman."

Jessie stared at him, then broke into laughter. "Think it's something you're going to like, do you?"

"Yes. I think so." Feodor gave a long, deliberate yawn. "I would like to try it again sometime."

Jessie kept a straight face. "Well you really weren't bad, you know. For your first time, I mean. I guess I ought to tell you."

"Good. I appreciate that."

He looked so terribly serious that Jessie couldn't hold back her laughter. "Feodor, you are a crazy Transylvanian. And if *that* was your first time, I don't think I can stand the second—when you really get the hang of it."

"I hope that is very soon."

She looked into his dark eyes and gave him a long,

searching kiss. "Oh, I think we can arrange that. I really think we can."

The horse was a sturdy farm animal, and Jessie rode along easily behind Feodor, her arms wrapped tightly about his back. After their lovemaking, she'd taken the time to rinse her clothes, and he'd carried them up the bank and spread them over a bush. They were still a little damp, but the cool cloth felt good against her skin.

Feodor kept to the far edge of the creek, under the trees. When they were close to the settlement, Jessie asked him to pull the horse deeper into the thicket, telling him she wanted to get off and talk with him for a few moments.

They dismounted and walked toward the creek, where Jessie stopped, pulled the revolver out of the waist of her denims, and inspected it in the light.

"Do you usually do away with your lovers after you use them up?" Feodor smiled.

Jessie laughed. "I didn't know you *were* used up. No, I left this out on the bank back there while we were, uh, occupied. I just wanted to make sure it didn't get any water or sand in it."

Feodor eyed the weapon with interest, and Jessie handed it to him.

"It is very beautiful pistol," he said. "What fine workmanship!" He turned it over and let the sun glint off the barrel. The polished peachwood grips were a perfect match for the light slate-gray finish.

"My father gave it to me," said Jessie, "and taught me how to use it. Started me out on a .44, but I practically had to lift the thing in two hands, and it kicked like a mule. So he had this made for me. It's a double-action .38 on a .44 frame, and fits me just right."

Feodor looked at her and handed back the weapon. "Jessica, your eyes sparkle when you talk about that pistol. I think it is the man who gave it to you who brings such pride to your eyes."

"Yes, you're very right about that." Jessie swallowed and looked away. She had shared a great deal with this man, and she trusted him. For a quick moment she felt like clinging to him and telling him all about Alex Starbuck—what he was and what he truly meant to her. And how greatly she missed him. She hesitated, though, knowing this wasn't the time and place for such confidences—even with a man like Feodor. The story of her father was one too tightly entwined with one she *couldn't* tell, one he might or might not understand.

She turned away for a moment and listened to the water trickling by in the creek below. "I'd like to tell you something," she said. "It's something you should know, Feodor. But I want to *ask* you something first."

Feodor looked puzzled. "Of course, Jessica."

She turned quickly and faced him. "Who approached you and your people to buy your land? Will you tell me?"

Feodor shrugged. "Certainly. Only I'm not sure who the man was. Gustolf handled all that."

"Do you know whether he was an American—or a European?"

"Oh, he was an American. Gustolf said that much."

"And he came out here and just—"

"No." Feodor frowned and shook his head. "No one came out here, Jessica. After the—after that creature killed the little girl, Gustolf waited, thinking perhaps it was not the curse of our homeland, but something else. Then, when the creature was seen again and again around the village, he was sure. He announced that we must move to another place. He went into Roster and asked around town for someone who could buy."

"And he found someone, I'll bet," Jessie said wryly.

"Yes he did. The lawman there told him who to see."

Jessie's eyes narrowed. "You mean Town Marshal Gaiter?"

"I don't know. That sounds right."

"Gaiter put Gustolf onto a buyer he just happened to know?"

"I think that's so."

Jessie let out a sigh. "Feodor, he didn't even go *talk* to Tom Bridger, did he? Let him know what he was thinking about doing?"

Feodor looked down at his boots. "No he didn't, Jessica. And I think you know why. You saw how he acted with you. Bridger was most kind to us when we settled here. Gustolf was . . . ashamed to face him."

"Bridger is dead, Feodor."

"What?" Feodor turned pale under his dark skin. "How did he—" He stopped and brought his lips firmly together. "I guess I already know that, don't I? Your eyes tell me how."

"He was shot down in the street. The night before Ki and I got to town."

Feodor gripped her shoulders. "Why are you telling me this, Jessica?"

"Because I want you to understand what's happening here. To you and your people."

"I can see what is happening. What do *you* know that I do not?"

"Someone wants to buy your land and buy it cheap. They're willing to do just about anything they can to get it. Including scaring you to death and killing off your people."

It suddenly dawned on Feodor what Jessie was trying to say. Concern, then anger and disbelief clouded his features. He turned abruptly away from her, jammed his hands in his pockets, and stared into the forest. "As I said before, I am a man who does not know what world he belongs to, Jessica, the old or the new. Perhaps it is a little of both." He turned then, and held her with his eyes. "That thing has killed two people. You were here, you saw what it did. Now you come to me and say there has been a shooting in town, a man who was our friend. That it has to do with buying land, and that this . . . man-wolf I do not believe in is a part of it. I do not understand this!"

"I don't either," Jessie told him. "Not yet, Feodor."

* * *

Ki rode out of the settlement as soon as there was light enough to see, leading his horse up the hill to the road back to Roster. Jessie would drop a casual word somewhere to let the settlers know he had business to attend to, and would likely be gone all day. She knew, though, that he had no intention of going into town.

He followed the dusty road a good mile, then swept his eyes carefully over the low horizon. When he was certain he was alone, he urged the mount into a run away from the road, toward the hills to the north. When the hills were nestled about him on either side, he slowed the mount to a walk and veered off west again, circling back toward the village. After a good half hour he slid off the horse, walked to the top of the hill, and went to his hands and knees. Ki allowed himself a satisfied smile. There was the settlement, not half a mile away against the dark row of trees that hid the creek. Closer, just below his perch, was the beginning of the wheatfields. They stretched out to the south as far as the eye could see, finally disappearing with the roll of the land. If he kept the line of hills between himself and the fields, he could ride for several miles before he cut back south again. That would give him cover, and allow him to look for tracks leading out of the fields. If he didn't find sign after a while, he'd cut into the wheat itself and look there. And if that didn't work, he would have to go west and trace past the creek.

It was a good day's job, he knew, unless he got lucky and spotted the animal's tracks right off. Logically, he knew he'd probably pick up the trail much sooner, starting from the place where the wolf had made its kills. Unfortunately, that spot was also in plain sight of the village, and both he and Jessie had decided that wouldn't be too good an idea.

Ki got off his horse and led it west, keeping his eyes to the ground. After only a few moments, he decided there was little chance of tracking anything over the grassy hills.

82

Even an Indian would have trouble finding sign here. He was far enough from the settlement now to risk moving out of the hills into the wheat, and he turned immediately to the south.

The sight of the fields heartened him at once. The soil between the tall, golden rows was full of tracks—mice, rabbits, birds, and all sorts of tiny creatures. If anything as big as a wolf had passed through, he'd have no trouble spotting its trail at once. He backtracked east for a while to make sure he hadn't missed anything in moving away from the settlement, then cut across the fields on a southwesterly course toward the creek.

Roughly halfway across the field, the thick rows ended abruptly. Ki stopped, surprised to come on such a place without warning. It was an outcropping of rock, a thirty-yard-wide circle, growing to head-high boulders in the center. Ki couldn't help thinking of an island rising up in the midst of a golden sea. The settlers, of course, had simply planted all around it, right to the edge of the stone.

Ki started around the area, staying off the rock itself, checking to see if any tracks led out of the field and onto the stony surface. A wolf wouldn't make its den in so small and accessible a place, but it might be attracted to the craggy—

The shot sounded sharp and flat, like a slap against the sky. A heavy slug snapped past his ear. Ki threw himself from his horse and came up running in a crouch, weaving for the cover of the wheat. The second shot chipped stone in his path, forcing him back. He jerked to the right, found a bullet there to meet him. He didn't try again—if he tried to get to the field, he knew he'd never make it alive. Turning on his heel, he sprinted for the rocky island. A bullet went right between his legs. Another tugged at his shirt. He leaped, throwing himself behind a low boulder.

Ki waited, hearing the panicked, receding hoofbeats of his horse as it raced away, probably back to its nice, safe stall in the Roster livery stable.

He let his breath and heartbeat slow to a manageable pace. A hard knot settled in his stomach, and he knew exactly what had happened. While he was tracking the wolf, someone had tracked him as well. Someone so good at what he was doing that none of Ki's senses had picked up an inkling of the person's presence. He'd been deliberately herded into the island of stone. Herded in alive. Whoever the hunter was, Ki knew any of the bullets that had passed him could have just as easily hit its mark. The tracker liked his work. He enjoyed teasing his prey before he came in for the kill...

★

Chapter 9

Ki quickly explored the wide circle of stones, and decided the place was both a fair sanctuary and an excellent trap. Unless his pursuer was a fool, which he didn't appear to be, it wasn't at all likely he'd leave the perfect cover of the wheatfield to hunt his quarry down. Why should he? If Ki didn't know by now that the man was a deadly shot, then *he* was a fool as well. If he so much as stuck his nose out of the rocky island, the hunter would shoot it off without blinking an eye.

Ki wasted no time in wondering who the man might be. Exactly what he intended was more important. Ki's mind moved rapidly over the possibilities, discarding those that seemed implausible or unlikely.

The man would not come in and get him; there was no need for that. Ki, in turn, would not bolt from cover. The hunter must know him, and understand his prey was not a frightened hare.

Assuming the man was alone, he could see at least half the perimeter of the circle at one time, without moving from cover. Which meant that Ki *could* try to escape—if he dared to risk his life on fifty-fifty odds.

He cursed himself for not thinking fast enough in the beginning. That had been an inexcusable error. Instead of using the rockpile for cover, he should have run right through it to the wheatfields beyond. Go in a hole and come out the other side. Leave the pursuer sniffing at the entry while you bound freely away. It was the basic ploy of any number of wild creatures—including, he reminded himself glumly, that supposedly frightened hare.

Ki leaned back and listened a long moment, then stared at the sun. It was a stalemate, then, or almost. He didn't have a gun, which his pursuer might or might not know. There was one in his saddlebag, along with several other weapons, including the corded *nunchaku* sticks, and a hardwood *bo* staff jointed in three sections. At the moment, of course, none of them would do him any good at all.

He still had the two *sai* tucked in his belt, and he could kill the man with them easily—if he could ever get to him. The *sai,* because of their great versatility, came close to being his favorite weapons. Essentially, they were blunted swords, roughly eighteen inches long, with two short prongs curling out from the hilt. He could drive the *sai* right through a man at any point on the body he chose, or throw it like a missile and stop a foe in his tracks.

Ki hefted one of the *sai,* and from the pocket of his leather jacket he selected several of the star-shaped *shuriken* throwing blades. He kept the *shuriken* in his left hand and the *sai* in his right, and moved out of his perch on his belly.

Resting on his haunches, Ki shifted his body in a slow circle, letting his eyes sweep the edge of the rocky wall that separated him from his enemy. Using his excellent ears and another sense that had no name, he searched for what he could not see. He waited, crouching under the sun. A hawk circled above. A snake caught a mouse in the wheat and cut off its squeal...

Ki watched the slow arc of the sun stretch the shadow of a small twig by his feet. An angry green fly sought him out and stung his cheek, but Ki didn't move. If the hunter

86

was trying to unnerve him, Ki could play that game just as well. The man was good, but Ki knew for certain he could *not* get close to the circle of rocks unheard. Ki would know he was there. Before he could jerk up from behind the boulders and bring his rifle to bear, Ki would take him. Kill him with the *sai*, or send one of the deadly throwing stars whirring into his throat. The man might keep his prey holed up in the trap, but he'd best not come in for a look at what he'd caught . . .

Sweat poured off his brow and stung his eyes, rolled down his chest and under his arms. Ki glanced at the twig and measured another long arc of the sun.

Gradually a new sound began to intrude on his senses. Ki listened, then came suddenly alert, straining to catch its meaning. It was a soft, rustling sound, almost a murmur like the wind. At first it came from one direction only, then gradually moved around him until it surrounded the stony isle. Suddenly, Ki knew exactly what it was. Raising slowly, he stretched his stiff muscles and moved silently to the edge of the rocks. Peering carefully between two slabs of stone, he saw them. Hundreds of prairie chickens were making their way through the wheatfield, busily plucking seeds and bugs from the soil.

He was almost certainly alone, then. If the shy, sensitive birds had seen the other man there, they would never have settled down to feed in such numbers. The hunter would have to be a stone. Ki was certain *he* could do it, but doubted the other man could. Still, there was no sense in being foolhardy now.

Bracing himself on the balls of his feet, he leaped over the protective stones, cut a low path for the high stalks of wheat, and rolled into cover. The birds scattered in fear, disappearing as quickly as they'd come.

Ki listened a long moment, then circled the stone island, weapons at the ready. He found the man's mark, saw how he'd watched him ride into the clearing, and knelt and fired the rifle. Ki bent to the earth and studied it carefully. What he saw didn't surprise him, but the discovery flooded him with shame and anger. He'd already suspected it might be true. Now he *knew* it was so. As soon as Ki had taken cover, the man had simply turned on his heel and walked away, leaving his prey to sweat it out alone. Ki had little choice in the matter, and the hunter well knew it. He'd had no intention of killing him. It was a joke, a deliberate humiliation, and something Ki swore he would not soon forget...

On the way to town, later that day, Ki sat silently in the saddle of his recovered horse, and glared into the late-afternoon sun.

"You're going to let that business get to you, aren't you?" said Jessie. "Don't guess I blame you, but there's nothing you can do about it now. You ought to know that."

"Yes," Ki said evenly, "I do know that, Jessie. And yes, I *am* going to let it get to me. Probably a great deal."

Jessie grinned, but not in Ki's direction. "What happened to your samurai calm, your, uh...acceptance of the karmic path?"

"Please..." Ki looked pained. "No Oriental wisdom right now. I am only half samurai, remember? The other half is Western. That is the half that is mad as hell because the Japanese half has been humiliated. I *know* it was Zascha who penned me in like a rabbit out there. I don't need any proof."

Jessie was silent a long moment. Behind the low rise ahead, she could see the small cluster of buildings that was Roster, and beyond that, the black smudge of the railroad drawn straight across the plain.

"Look," she said finally, "are you trying to tag something else on this? Besides a sorehead's bad joke?"

Ki gazed straight ahead.

Ki shrugged. "True enough. I don't know, Jessie. Zascha is a troublemaker. He was stirring up the villagers against us last night, but before we got here, I'm sure it was something else. He is against everything. And he's not the only man in the settlement who's ready to sell out. Just the loudest." Ki paused a moment, then went on, "I neglected to mention that he sent a couple of his friends after me last night."

"I noticed the bruise on your mouth," Jessie said. "I figured you'd tell me about it sooner or later." She shook her head and sighed. "*Someone's* involved in this business. I don't mean Zascha or any of the villagers. Just someone. And whoever it is, he knows exactly what goes on out there." She'd already told Ki what Feodor had to say about when the trouble with wolves had started. "That little girl was killed after the cartel started sniffing around after land. I don't know how they're doing it, Ki, but our old friends from Europe have got a hand in this."

The Morgan Dollar was going strong, but there was little sign of other activity on Main. Jessie and Ki left their horses at the livery, then walked across the street to the marshal's office before going to the hotel. Marshal Gaiter was reading a week-old Kansas City paper by a kerosene lamp when the pair walked in. He looked up from the yellow pool of light as if something had just died and he'd gotten a good whiff of it.

"Like to help you folks," he said too quickly, reaching for his hat. "Just closin' up to go to supper."

"Wouldn't think of keeping you long," said Jessie. "Just need a little help, is all."

"Yeah, well . . ." Gaiter took a quick glance at Ki's casual stance in the doorway and settled back in the chair with a frown. "I got a minute, I guess. What can I do for you?"

"We want to talk to Lucy Jordan," said Jessie.

Gaiter's eyes narrowed. "Wh-what for?"

"She tried to kill me on the train. Remember? There are a couple of things I'd like to ask her."

"Well, it's gettin' kinda late. Might be in the morning'd be better."

"Right now would be fine, though, wouldn't it?" Ki gave him his friendliest smile. It stretched the skin as taut as new leather over his cheekbones, narrowed the dark almond eyes, and scared the hell out of Gaiter.

"Sure, I guess it's all right..." He wet his lips and looked nervously at Jessie. "'Course, *I* gotta be there if you do. Talk to her, I mean."

Jessie raised an eyebrow and tipped back the brim of her Stetson. "Suits me, Marshal. Can't see why you'd want to, though."

"The girl's got rights, you know. She, ah...ain't been tried and convicted."

Jessie glanced quickly at Ki and smiled at Gaiter. "Lucy's real lucky to have a lawman like you around, Marshal."

"Well, I'm just doin' my job..." he muttered darkly.

"I understand that, and I appreciate it. Maybe you're right."

"About what?"

"Talking to Lucy Jordan. We can always get with her later." Jessie perched one hip on Gaiter's desk. "Why don't you and me talk some first?"

"Uh, what about?" Gaiter flushed and chewed on his beard. The nearby curve of Jessie's thigh in snug-fitting denim made him decidedly uneasy.

"How about land buying?"

"Don't know a lot about it." The marshal's watery eyes flicked quickly down to his hands.

"That's funny. We heard you did. Old Gustolf, out at the settlement, came into town a while back looking for someone who might be interested in buying land. You were the one who found someone he could talk to."

"Don't remember a thing about anything like—" Gaiter caught himself and grinned. "Oh, yeah, maybe I did. See a lot of people in my job."

"I thought you didn't know any of the settlers," Ki put in.

"Don't!" snapped Gaiter. "Maybe talked to one of 'em

once. Hell, I don't know." He clamped his jaw shut and glared at them both. "Listen, what the hell is this?"

"Who did you tell Gustolf to talk to?"

"Don't recall. That was some time ago."

Jessie widened her eyes in surprise. "You mean there are *that* many land buyers in Roster? I wouldn't have guessed!"

"Now listen, Miss Starbuck—"

"No, *you* listen." Gaiter started to get up but Jessie stopped him with a finger cocked like a pistol. "You and I can play games if you like, but it might be better for both of us if we don't. I can't prove anything right yet, but I have an idea you *might* be mixed up in something a little too big for you to swallow. If I'm right—"

Gaiter shot to his feet. "Just—get out of here. Both of you! I've took just about all of this business I want to. I'm the law in this town, Miss High-an'-Mighty Starbuck, and it don't make no difference who you are or how much money you got. You can't just stomp in and insult whoever you please!"

The old man was shaking, and Jessie knew there was more to it than anger. "I can, you know," she said softly, "you're wrong."

"About what?"

"I *can* walk in and insult anyone I want. Because I'm a Starbuck."

Gaiter went red. "Well, goddamn—!"

"Only I wouldn't, Marshal. Because I don't believe in abusing power. That goes for local officials on up to very rich ladies, by the way. And I don't have any respect for someone who does. What I can do and what I *will* do is use whatever power I have to see that murderers are brought to justice. Here, or anywhere else."

Gaiter blinked. "Jesus, when did we start talkin' about murder?"

"Just now. Two people out at the settlement and Tom Bridger here in town. If you're mixed up with anyone who has blood on their hands, I'll see that it rubs off on you."

"Now hold on there . . ." Gaiter raised a hand. "You are *way* out of line, lady."

"Good," Jessie said firmly. "Then it won't bother you if I walk over to the telegraph office and bring about a dozen federal marshals and judges into Roster. Real sharp-eyed boys who'll go over this place from the town drunk on up."

Gaiter looked right into Jessie's flashing green eyes and decided she might not be bluffing at all. He wasn't sure just what money could do, but he had an idea it might do plenty. For the moment, at least, he wasn't sure Jessica Starbuck couldn't call Rutherford B. Hayes himself down to Roster.

"Well, Marshal?" asked Jessie. "You think maybe you'd like to help us out some?"

Gaiter looked pained, then suddenly relaxed and grinned past her shoulder.

Jessie turned around and saw why.

"Good evening, Miss Starbuck. Marshal." Torgler smiled and tipped his hat, let his eyes flick over the room, and somehow missed Ki completely. "Another pleasant evening, isn't it? I hope you're enjoying your stay here, dear lady."

"Not too much, thanks." Jessie gave him a narrow, thoughtful look. "How about you?"

"Miss Starbuck came by to see Lucy—ah, our prisoner," Gaiter put in quickly.

Torgler raised a brow. "Oh, is that so? May I inquire as to why, Miss Starbuck?"

Jessie returned his polite smile in kind. "May I inquire as to why you're *inquiring,* Mr. Torgler?"

"Of course. Miss Lucy Jordan is my client. I have been retained to represent her."

Jessie tried to hide her expression, but Torgler caught it and looked pleased. "You're a—an attorney?" Jessie looked up at the ceiling. "Now why didn't I guess that right off? Just who retained you, Mr. Torgler?"

"Why, Miss Jordan herself."

"And I guess you'd object if I wanted to ask her a few questions."

"Oh, I'm afraid I'd *have* to, ma'am." Torgler looked as if turning Jessie down hurt him deeply. "Since you are the plaintiff charging Miss Jordan with alleged assault—"

"*Alleged* assault?" Ki stood up straight.

"Yes." Torgler turned on him with eyes cold as ice. "Miss Jordan is being held, sir. She has yet to see a judge, hear formal charges, or be tried—if she *is* to be tried." He turned abruptly to Jessie. "Of course you can't talk to her. That would hardly be fair to Miss Jordan, now would it?"

"It—" Jessie swallowed her anger and looked from Torgler to Gaiter. The marshal was grinning like an ape, but his smile faded under Jessie's withering glance. "Ki, come on. I don't guess we have any more business here. I'll be seeing you again, Mr. Torgler."

Torgler's eyes almost closed. "I do hope so, dear lady."

Jessie turned and stormed out of the room, Ki at her heels. As she stalked across the street toward the hotel, two young boys from the café passed her, heading back for the marshal's office. Both were loaded down with trays covered with white linen napkins, and Jessie picked up the tantalizing odors of thick, sizzling steaks, mashed potatoes, and peach cobbler. Two bottles of the best whiskey in Roster jiggled in the second boy's coverall pockets.

"Will you look at that!" Jessie stopped and glared, fury clouding her features. "Torgler and *poor* little Lucy and the marshal are having a picnic, right there in the damn jailhouse! It's a good thing I don't have a couple of sticks of dynamite and a match, Ki. I'd be sorely tempted to use 'em!"

★

Chapter 10

It was after six when Ki tapped lightly on Jessie's door, and the two wandered out of the hotel and across the street to the Silver Bell Café. The evening was still bright under a luminous summer sky. The sun wouldn't flatten into Colorado for another two hours, and the day would linger on after that. Jessie hadn't eaten since five that morning, and she felt as hollow as a drum. She'd missed the noonday meal at the village, being somewhat occupied with Feodor and not even thinking about food. When the big steak arrived, she worked through it with a will, polishing her plate clean with a thick piece of bread.

Ki watched in amazement. He was a hearty enough eater, but no match for Jessie in one of her ravenous moods. "I'm glad this place wasn't out of food," he said soberly. "It would be embarrassing to watch you shoot your way through the kitchen."

"Don't laugh, friend." Jessie gave him a stern, reproachful look. "If Torgler and his crew had cornered all the steaks in town, I might have done just that." Jessie leaned back in her chair and let out a breath. "Ki, I think there was a lot that Tom Bridger could have told us about what's going on in this place. The longer we hang around Roster, the easier it is to see why they killed him. If you ask me, everyone in town's for hire. It'd be a lot easier for Torgler if they all wore price tags on their collars."

The occupants of the other two tables were eyeing Jessie curiously. She glared them down and leaned across to Ki. "We know he's bought Gaiter, and God knows who else. There's Lucy, of course, and likely a bunch of assorted gunmen like those two on the train."

"We are not entirely without help if we need it," Ki grinned. "Remember that swarm of federal marshals and judges you threatened to toss at Gaiter?"

Jessie didn't laugh. "Gaiter'll buy that. A man like Torgler knows better." She had learned that lesson the hard way after Alex Starbuck's murder. The law was next to useless in this kind of fight. The cartel was playing for high stakes, and one of the deadliest weapons it brought into play was its seemingly bottomless purse. Small fry like Gaiter, and even professional assassins like Lucy Jordan put no strain at all on the organization's funds. The cartel operated on a grander scale than that—buying the men who *made* the laws, as well as those who enforced them. Wherever money talked, the cartel opened its pockets. Jessie was well aware of the fact that high-placed men across the country— men in business, the military, the railroads, even in Washington itself—were in the pay of European interests. And sometimes, even the most honest and iron-willed men who *couldn't* be bought with money and the promise of power could be broken to the cartel's will in other ways. When a child's in danger, or it's hinted that a lovely young wife might be maimed through some unfortunate accident, a man can be persuaded to change his mind.

And that, thought Jessie, was perhaps the ugliest and most menacing aspect of the cartel's power. How do you fight an organization of ruthless and powerful men who will use any weapon at their command—without becoming what they are yourself? It was a question she had asked herself more than once.

Night was swiftly drawing a curtain over the plains when Jessie and Ki left the café. Jessie had said little since supper, and Ki knew what was gnawing at her mind. He felt it too—as if things they couldn't see were pressing in around them, and there was nothing they could do to keep them away.

"If I was a drinker," said Jessie, "I think right now would be a good time to open up a bottle. Don't guess it would solve a thing, though, would it?"

"Not a great deal," said Ki. "Jessie, in the morning I think we should go back out to the settlement and talk to Gustolf and the others. We know a lot about what's happening here and who's behind it."

Jessie shook her head. "Those folks don't want to hear about international cartels and crooked sheriffs. They've got a werewolf on their hands, Ki—or think they do, which works out to about the same thing."

"We know that's not true."

Jessie stopped and faced him. "But we don't know much else, do we? Like how you get a wolf to tear out a man's throat. *We* don't have any answers, and that old man has all he needs. He's going to sell out for sure, Ki, and likely get down on his knees and *thank* our mysterious land buyer for giving pennies on the dollar."

"And that mysterious buyer will turn out to be Torgler."

Jessie looked pained. "Uh-huh. One of his flunkies made the offer when Gaiter sent Gustolf over to him. But you can be sure Torgler himself will be on hand to close the deal. He'll have the cash right with him, waiting for the proper time to pop up out there. Which I'd say is just about now, wouldn't you? With a brand-new death in the village?"

Ki didn't answer. Jessie stopped and stretched, brushed hair out of her eyes, and gazed into the gathering dark. There was a light in the marshal's office and a pool of yellow around the door of the Morgan Dollar. The rest of the town was silent and deserted. As Jessie watched, a shadow stepped off Gaiter's porch and stalked into the street.

"Who is it?" asked Jessie. "Torgler, going after more whiskey and steaks?"

"No, it's the marshal," Ki said after a moment. "I think he's making his evening rounds."

"I didn't know he bothered," Jessie said acidly. "Gaiter pretending he's a lawman is about the—" She caught herself and sighed. "I've really let that man get to me, haven't I? For some reason, Ki, he angers me more than Torgler or Lucy Jordan. Maybe it's because he's such a little fish in all this mess, and doesn't even know it. Slip him a handful of shiny gold coins, and he thinks he's—"

"Jessie—" Ki's steel grip brought her quickly out of her thoughts. "Jessie, turn around and get back to the hotel—*now!*"

"Ki? What *is* it?"

"I don't know," he snapped. "Just do it." His face was a rigid mask. Black eyes darted past her, searching out the night. Jessie knew that look and didn't question him again. She turned on her heels and broke into a run down the wooden sidewalk.

"Gaiter!" Ki shouted suddenly behind her. *"Look out!"*

Jessie turned. Her boot caught a loose board and sent her sprawling. In the smallest part of a second she saw it happen . . . the enormous gray shadow sprang past Ki out of the alley . . . Gaiter stood frozen in the street . . . his hand snaked to his waist and three quick explosions brightened the night . . . the thing leaped off the ground with a snarl and slammed him in the chest . . . Gaiter shrieked . . . the creature tore at him, shook its great head . . .

Jessie blinked, and it was over.

"Jessie!" Ki came up out of a crouch.

"I'm all right. I think . . ." She pulled herself up and went to him, one eye on the darkened alley. Half a dozen men

98

came out of the Morgan Dollar and stared cautiously in their direction.

"Bring a lantern over here," shouted Ki. "Hurry!" Several of the men started toward them. Two ran back into the saloon yelling for lights. Ki bent over the marshal and struck a match.

"Oh, God!" Jessie's stomach turned and she quickly looked away. Gaiter's throat was completely gone. His face was twisted in horror.

Ki tossed the match away and stood. "You saw it?"

"Yes, I saw it, all right. Ki, that thing was too big to be a wolf!"

"It was a wolf," he assured her. Ki gripped her shoulders and gave her a long hard look. "You saw it, Jessie, and so did I. It was a wolf. It wasn't anything else."

Four men strode up, glanced curiously at Ki and Jessie, and squatted over the marshal. A tall young man with a lantern pushed them aside and stared down at the body. "Jesus Christ, it's Jack Gaiter!" He handed the lantern to another man and walked over to Ki. "You see what happened, mister? God*damn*—looks like a grizzly got to him."

"A wolf," said Ki. "A very *large* wolf." He glanced at the badge on the man's vest. "You are a lawman?"

"Sort of," he grunted. "I'm Mac Delbert, an' I know who you and the lady are. I did a little deputy work for Jack—what there was of it." He squinted narrowly at Ki. "A *wolf?* You sure, mister?"

"Del, get a look at this!" The man with the lantern was standing at the edge of the alley, and the others were crowded around him. The deputy walked past Jessie and Ki, and squatted on his heels.

"Holy shit!" he said between his teeth. "'Scuse me, ma'am." He poked a finger at the big print in the dirt. "Frank," he called over his shoulder, "get a couple of boys with Winchesters and lanterns and see if you can figure where that thing took off to. You ain't goin' to find nothin',

99

so don't go shootin' in the dark." He stood and looked at Ki. "Gaiter got off a couple of shots. How close was that thing to him?"

"I saw it," said Jessie. "The animal was right on top of him."

Delbert looked at her. "You sure, lady?"

"Of course I'm sure!"

Ki nodded soberly and turned to face her. "I saw the thing too, Jessie. I think what the deputy's saying is that there is no blood on the ground. If Marshal Gaiter hit the animal even once with a .44—"

"Ki—" Jessie shook her head in disbelief. "I *saw* it! He practically poked the muzzle down that thing's throat!"

Delbert chewed his lip a moment, then walked over and found Gaiter's pistol, broke open the chamber, and closed it again. Holding the weapon at a slight angle, he fired two shots into the ground. Dirt coughed up, leaving two neat grooves in the street. "Nothing's wrong with his bullets," he said. "Guess you folks didn't see as clear as you figured." Jessie started to protest, but Delbert held up a hand. "Things don't always look like they seem, you go through something like that, ma'am."

"Yes, I—guess you're right," Jessie said lamely.

Delbert nodded. "You folks mind goin' over to the office a minute? Someone's got to write this up, and I guess that's me. We could do it in the morning, I s'pose..."

"No, now'll be just fine," said Jessie.

"Be right over, then. Soon's I get things kinda cleaned up here." The deputy left them, and Ki and Jessie turned back up the street. As soon as the man was out of hearing, Jessie stopped Ki and faced him squarely.

"I *know* what I saw," she said fiercely, "and so do you. Gaiter *couldn't* have missed, Ki. Not at that range."

"No, I know that, Jessie. But he did, didn't he? And he wasn't shooting blanks."

"I know what I saw," she muttered.

"Maybe we'd better start using some of Gustolf's silver bullets.

Jessie's green eyes flashed. "Ki, that is *not* very funny!"

"It's what you were thinking."

"Maybe. But I had the good sense not to say it." She stepped off the street onto the board sidewalk and into Gaiter's front office. The marshal's chair was pulled away from his desk, just as he'd left it moments before. A dim lantern swung from the ceiling. Jessie wrinkled her nose at the smell of stale whiskey and steak grease, stalked across the office, and opened the rear door. There was a short hallway and a single cell. Another lantern hung from the low ceiling. In the hall was a table full of plates, congealed steak bones, and half-empty bottles of good bourbon. The cell door was open and Lucy Jordan was gone.

Jessie stood in the hall with her hands on her hips. "How come I'm not at all surprised, Ki? The marshal's dead, Lucy Jordan's escaped, and guess who left the party early? Our good friend Torgler. *Damn!*" Jessie kicked an empty bottle and sent it shattering across the floor.

"An amazing set of coincidences," Ki agreed solemnly.

Jessie took one last look around the room, marched past Ki, and perched on the edge of Gaiter's desk. "He did it, you know," she flared. "I don't know how, but he did it. The marshal had served his purpose, and Torgler *knew* we saw right through him. So he shut Gaiter up and let Lucy out!"

Ki thought a moment. "Why not get rid of Lucy Jordan as well?"

"Maybe he did," shrugged Jessie. "He couldn't very well do it here, could he? Even the good folks of Roster wouldn't buy too many bodies showing up in one night. You know what, though? I don't think Torgler'd touch Lucy Jordan. She's much too good at what she does." Jessie made a face. "No use firing a good employee who can still put in an honest day's work for you. Anyway—" Jessie stopped as

101

heavy bootsteps sounded outside and the marshal's deputy stepped through the door.

"Appreciate you folks comin' by," he said evenly. "This won't take but a minute." He looked at Jessie and Ki and shook his head. "We didn't get us any wolf, which don't much surprise me. Most of them boys wasn't too anxious to look real hard in the dark and—" The deputy cut himself off and looked curiously from Ki to Jessie. "Why do I get the idea there's somethin' goin' on here I don't know?"

"Because there is," Jessie said flatly. "Your cell back there's kind of empty, Mr. Delbert. Someone let your prisoner loose while Gaiter was making his rounds."

"Aw, hell..." Delbert looked as though he had a bad taste in his mouth. "Jack sure left me a barrel of snakes, didn't he? Who you reckon got in here?"

Jessie stood and hitched up her belt. "No one had to get in," she said blandly. "Someone was already here. Lucy's attorney, Mr. Torgler. When Ki and I left a while ago, they were all having a party."

"Is that so? You see 'em?"

"We saw all the food and whiskey going in. Of course, if you go talk to Torgler, you'll find he likely left before the marshal, and was somewhere else entirely."

Delbert took off his hat and scratched his head. "Funny you should say that, ma'am—"

"What's so funny about it?"

"'Cause it's true, Miss Starbuck. One of the boys knew Torgler was a friend of Jack Gaiter's and went over to the hotel to tell him. Woke him up out of a sound sleep. Said the man was shaken real good. Couldn't believe Jack was dead, 'cause he'd just had supper with him." Delbert paused and looked at Jessie. "Listen, you're not tryin' to say Mr. Torgler let that little gal out of here, are you?"

Jessie glanced at the ceiling. "Now why would I want to do that?"

"I don't know," Delbert said narrowly. "From what I

102

hear, he's a real fine man. And he sure did think some of old Jack!"

"We know," said Jessie.

"Not all of it, you don't," Delbert told her. "He's footin' the whole funeral out of his own pocket. Told old McTavish he wanted a brand-new two-hundred-dollar coffin in on the next train from Kansas City, and a fifty-dollar suit. You can't hardly do more than that for a man, now can you?"

★

Chapter 11

Jessie walked out of the hotel, squinted into the early morning light, and stared in amazement at Main. For a moment she decided she'd somehow gotten up in the wrong town. The normally sleepy street was swarming with people. Horses were packed together at the hitching posts, and wagons rattled by, forcing townfolk to scatter.

"Good Lord," said Jessie, "what do you suppose it is, Ki? A gold rush or the circus come to town?"

"Closer to the circus," Ki said glumly. "Look there, past the livery." He touched Jessie's arm and guided her to the end of the wooden sidewalk. Raw wood posts had been driven into the dirt, and half the alley was roped off. A crowd of citizens three deep were shouldering each other aside to get a peek. Inside the rope stood Mac Delbert, the lean part-time deputy they'd met the night before. His ragged denims and old jacket had been replaced by a shiny black suit, white shirt, string tie, and a red silk vest that had seen better days. A battered, quickly brushed derby was perched on his head. On the livery wall behind Delbert was a hastily scrawled sign in bright red paint:

SEE THE GIGANIC WOLF TRACS OF THE
BEEST THAT KILT JACK GAITER!!!

"Oh, my God," moaned Jessie, "I can't believe this!"

"What you can believe," Ki said wryly, "is that Delbert is already running for town marshal."

"He'll likely win, too. Come on, let's get some breakfast before I lose my appetite."

After another half-block, Jessie saw she'd spoken too soon. The sight behind the plate glass window of the McTavish Undertaking Parlour was anything but conducive to a hearty breakfast. The late Jack Gaiter was laid out stiff as a board on a red plush couch. His suit was brand new, and Jessie was sure he'd never worn one nearly so fine standing up. A shiny silver star was pinned to his chest, and a dove-gray ascot circled his ruined throat. McTavish had made a real effort to bring Gaiter's color back to his face, and had evidently gotten carried away with his work. Jessie tried to find a more charitable way to describe the man, but her first thought stuck. The marshal looked a lot like a dead clown.

To top off the scene, the enterprising undertaker had cut out a picture and pasted it against the glass, a catalog engraving of the fine plush coffin Torgler had ordered from Kansas City—price tag included. The whole business made Jessie furious.

"Well, good morning, Miss Starbuck. Terrible tragedy, wasn't it?"

Jessie recognized the voice and turned around, making no effort to hide her anger. "This medicine show your doing, Torgler? It's sure got your mark on it."

Torgler's cold blue eyes sparkled like ice. "Why, whatever do you mean, dear lady?"

"You know exactly what I mean. And for God's sake, please don't waste your good manners on me. We understand each other perfectly, mister."

"Why, yes, I suppose we do, don't we?"

"Exactly. And it's not over yet. You just keep that in mind."

"Oh, I will, Miss Starbuck. I most certainly will."

Jessie held his gaze, but shuddered inside. There was nothing behind the man's eyes. It was like looking into the windows of a cold empty house where nobody lived. She was relieved when two prim ladies elbowed her aside to get to Torgler.

"Oh, my," gushed the fatter of the pair, "what a noble gesture, Mr. Torgler, honoring our marshal like this. You have made Roster *so* proud!"

"Oh, so proud indeed!" echoed the second.

"A pleasure on my part," said Torgler, tipping the brim of his hat. "The very least one can do for a fallen warrior."

"How well said," agreed the first lady, shaking her head at Gaiter's still form. "Such a fine, fine man. He'll be sorely missed in Roster..."

Jessie couldn't stand it any longer. No one in Roster had even *noticed* the marshal until he appeared in McTavish's front window—certainly not these two biddies.

"Hey, hold it a minute, folks!" Jessie stepped forward and raised her hands to get the crowd's attention. "I think we owe Marshal Gaiter more than just a coffin and a fine funeral. I think we owe him the satisfaction of knowing this kind of thing will never happen in Roster again." She paused to make certain every head was turned her way. "That's why I'm offering two hundred and fifty U.S. dollars for every freshly killed wolf hide I see nailed to that livery wall!"

The crowd stared at Jessie, then broke into a ragged cheer. Hats flew into the air, and men rushed down the street to spread the news. Torgler went livid. His cold eyes bored into Jessie and he turned on his heels and stalked away.

Jessie laughed out loud, tossed her hair back over her shoulders, and let Ki guide her through the crowd into the street. *"Now* I've got an appetite, Ki. Let's get some breakfast inside us and ride out to the settlement. I am *not* going to let him get away with this. If I have to sit on Gustolf myself, he isn't going to sell out to Torgler!"

The café was relatively empty, since nearly everyone in town was out milling in the street. Jessie ordered a breakfast steak, hotcakes, and potatoes, and downed two cups of coffee before the feast arrived.

"All right," she said finally, slicing into her steak, "you haven't said two words since we sat down. You don't approve, do you?"

"Do I have to answer that?"

"I don't think so. I'm getting the message real clearly."

"It has nothing to do with approving, Jessie. You are in danger from that man. He wants to see you dead. Now you have given him further reason."

Jessie stared, quickly swallowed a bite of potatoes, and washed it down with coffee. "Good grief, Ki. Are you serious? Do you honestly think the man could hate me any more than he does now?" She shook her head and waved a fork in his face. "He used Marshal Gaiter, then murdered him. I don't know how he did it, but you know as well as I do that he's guilty. He also turned that redheaded assassin loose again, and I'm not too happy about that. And what did he get for it? My God—he's the town hero of Roster!"

"You see," Ki said soberly, "you are giving me all my own arguments, Jessie. There is only one thing that could cause a man like Torgler to act rashly. A blow to his pride. You have given him good reason to strike back."

"He's already *got* good reason."

Ki shrugged. "It's over. There is no need to talk about it."

Jessie looked up at his tone, and reached across the table to touch his hand. "Ki, I'm sorry. I know you've got my best interests at heart, and I guess it was a foolish thing to do. All right?"

Ki couldn't stand up against her saucy grin. His somber face broke into a smile, and Jessie laughed. "You have to admit it was a good idea, now don't you? If there's a wolf within a hundred miles of Roster, it'll head north for Canada real soon. You finished? Let's get the horses and get out of here."

Ki nodded and left money on the table. Jessie downed the last of her coffee and made her way through the tables for the door. The street had cleared some outside, but there was still a crowd in front of McTavish's window.

As they turned toward the stables, Jessie saw Feodor approaching on horseback. She waved and called out, "Feodor! Over here!"

Feodor waved back and turned his horse in to the hitching post before the café. Jessie started for him, and had taken two quick steps before a bullet snapped past her head and shattered the window of the café. Jessie turned, startled, and heard Ki's hoarse warning a split second before his body hit her hard and slammed her to the sidewalk. Bright showers of glass sprinkled the street. A woman screamed somewhere, and a man cursed inside the café. Ki rolled Jessie roughly off the sidewalk and into the dirt. Three rapid shots followed the first, plowing up sand and stitching a path behind him. Ki came up in a crouch, covering Jessie's body and quickly scanning the building across the street.

"Get down!" Feodor shouted. Ki hugged the dirt as a shot parted his hair and Feodor's rifle opened up. Ki saw a rifle barrel disappear from a dark window, and sprinted across the street under Feodor's covering fire. Jessie came to her feet and scrambled around the side of Feodor's mount.

"Did he make it all right?"

"He's inside," snapped Feodor. "Keep down, Jessica!" He leveled another shell into the Winchester and fired into the window where the gunman had disappeared. Keeping one eye on the building, he clawed a handful of shells out of his saddlebag and stuffed them in his jacket. "I'm going around back," he told Jessie. "If your friend flushes him out, maybe I can get him when he makes a run for it."

"Good idea," Jessie agreed. "Glad you showed up when you—"

Feodor stopped in mid-stride. "Jessica, where do you think you're going?"

"With you. What do you think I'm going to do? Stay here?"

"It seems like a good idea. That gunman was after *you,* you know."

Jessie's eyes flashed. "You sound just like Ki! Everyone thinks they have to take care of poor old Jessie!"

Feodor gave her a narrow look and started across the street. "Now why would anyone think that?"

Jessie caught up with him and glared. "Making love to me does *not* give you branding privileges, mister. It'd be a good idea if you remembered that!"

Feodor didn't even bother to answer.

Ki edged quickly up the narrow wooden stairs, his slipper-clad feet making no sound at all. The door at the top was open. Fancy gold lettering on frosted glass read LANSDALE & SHINER, INC., FERTILIZER & FEED. Ki flattened against the wall, listened a brief moment, then threw himself into the room and rolled for cover. The small office was empty, but the floor by the far window was littered with empty brass casings. Ki turned and swept his eyes across the room. There was a back window, leading to a narrow walkway over the alley. He grasped the two three-pronged *sai* in one hand, moved a leg over the sill, and peered up the side of the building. The gunman could have jumped into the alley, but Ki figured he hadn't. It was a long drop onto a pile of splintered crates and broken glass. The roof was the easy way, with no chance of breaking a leg or running into pursuers coming around from the street. Ki thrust the weapons into his belt, grabbed the high coping along the window, and jerked himself onto the flat roof. He came to his feet in a roll, the weapons already in his hands. Something moved on the roof next door. Ki threw himself flat as the rifle fired twice. He jerked to the left, then reversed himself and came to his feet where the rifleman wouldn't expect him. Another shot rang out, but Ki wasn't there. He whirled the *sai* in his hand and set it flying. A silver blur flashed through the air. The gunman threw up the rifle and cried out, stunbled back and nearly fell, then limped to cover under a pile of new lumber.

Ki muttered a curse and leaped the space between his building and the next. The gunman wasn't hurt, the *sai* had only nicked him. And it wasn't a *him* at all, damn it, it was the redheaded assassin Torgler had so kindly released from jail. She was wearing a man's clothing, but Ki wasn't blind. He'd been shot at before, and none of the gunmen had ever looked anything like Lucy.

He went to his hands and knees behind a tar barrel and peered cautiously around the side. "Give it up," he called out. "There's no place to go, Lucy!"

"I'm hurt real bad . . ." Lucy said softly. "What the hell did you cut me with?"

"Come out of there and I'll show you. And you're not hurt, so don't give me that."

"Ha! Fat chance. You'll *kill* me is what you'll do. That lady friend of yours wants me dead!" Lucy wailed.

"Lucy," Ki said wearily, "forget the little-girl act. I am not the late town marshal." Ki waited. "Lucy? Give it up. All right?"

Lucy didn't answer. Ki wasn't about to swallow a trick like that. She was still right there, behind the pile of lumber. If she tried to get off the roof, he'd hear her for sure. If she stayed where she was—

Lucy cried out, and Ki came suddenly alert. He cocked his head to listen, realized with a start what was wrong, and scrambled desperately for the stack of boards. The scream hadn't come from there at all—it had come from somewhere else!

Ki froze in his tracks and cursed himself for a fool. Lucy was gone. There was a small trapdoor behind the lumber leading down into the building. She'd tripped on the stepladder or he'd never have heard her at all.

He flew down the ladder, hardly touching the rungs. The ladder went farther than he thought, clear down to street level. The building was a dark, two-story warehouse and stank to high heaven. Ki soon saw the reason. The warehouse belonged to the office he'd entered next door. The room was full of big bales marked LANSDALE & SHINER. Ki walked cautiously around a corner. A dusty beam of light from high above glanced off the floor. Ki went to his knees and listened. A rat scampered by on a rafter. Sounds drifted in from the street. Other than that . . .

Lucy moved, a shadow to the right less than twenty yards away. "Don't!" Ki warned her. "I'll use it, Lucy!"

The girl turned, leveled a pistol at him, and squeezed off two quick shots. Ki threw the *sai* into darkness and dove for cover. Bales exploded behind him and showered him with foul-smelling dirt. He jerked to his feet and moved fast. Hazy light flooded the room and he caught a quick glimpse of Lucy Jordan slipping through an outside door. Ki ran, found the street, and jerked to a stop, searching both ends of Main. He saw her then, keeping to the board sidewalk and racing for the far end of town like a deer. Ki went after her, gaining on her fast. "Stop that girl!" he called out. "Stop her!"

Men and women turned in the street to stare. "Stop her!" Ki yelled angrily. "She's a killer!"

Suddenly, Lucy disappeared in a small crowd of men clustered in front of the Morgan Dollar. Half a second later she burst out the other side, a different Lucy Jordan altogether.

"Rape! Rape!" she shrieked at the top of her lungs. "Oh, God help me—the Chinaman's gone and *raped* me!"

Ki came to an abrupt halt. A few of the men turned on him and glared. Some had trouble taking their eyes off Lucy. She'd ripped her blouse clear down to her waist, baring one delicious breast altogether, and offering a provocative peek at the other.

"Get him!" a hefty cowhand bellowed. "Get the goddamn chink!" One man took up the cry, then another, and the whole crowd surged toward Ki. A dozen men boiled out of the saloon. They had no idea where they were going, but it sounded like something to do.

Ki turned on his heel and ran down Main toward the tracks. The men behind him shouted out warnings ahead. Helpful citizens raced to cut him off. Ki cursed under his breath and bolted into an alley.

"Hold it right there, mister!"

Two hammers clicked louder than any Ki had ever heard. He raised his arms fast and stared into the cavernous double bores of a Greener shotgun. A calm blue eye squinted back from over the barrels.

"This is a mistake," Ki said evenly. "Be careful with that thing."

"Yeah, an' you're the one made it!" the man snapped.

"By God, you tell 'im, Sy!"

"If he moves, shoot his yeller eyes out!"

Men crowded into the alley from both sides. Ki backed up against the wall. One man drew his Colt and emptied it into the air. That started the others, and the alley soon sounded like a small war.

Deputy Mac Delbert shouldered his way through the crowd, Jessie and Feodor close on his heels. Ki breathed a sigh of relief. Delbert held up his hands to stop the noise.

"Pete, Joe Bob—what in the *hell* you think you're doin'?" He looked about the circle in disgust. "You all get on back to drinkin' or whatever 'twas you was doin'."

"Mac," blurted a man at the rear, "this feller here—"

"—hasn't done shit. Now go on, *git!*" The men muttered their disappointment, turning their anger from Ki to the deputy. "Sorry about this, mister," said Delbert. "You're all right, I guess."

"Fine," said Ki. "Anyone see which way Lucy Jordan went?"

Delbert grinned. "Hell, I reckon every man in town can

113

likely tell you that. Never seen such—uh, sorry, ma'am." He looked sheepishly at Jessie and bit his jaw.

Jessie ignored him. "South, I think, Ki. Someone was yelling down Main about his horse."

Ki nodded and turned on Delbert. "How many men can you get together fast?"

Delbert looked blank. "Uh—get together for what?"

"To go after Lucy Jordan! Deputy, that girl is a cold-blooded—"

"Yeah, I know." Delbert waved him off. "Wish I could help, but I ain't really a deputy no more—since there ain't no one to be deputy to." Delbert stopped and scratched his head. "An' if there was, it'd be a town marshal, wouldn't it? Which means I got no business twice-removed goin' after that gal, do I? Thing is—"

Ki wasn't listening. He was already stalking angrily toward the stable, half hoping one of the patrons of the Morgan Dollar would get in his way...

★

Chapter 12

Jessie deliberately hurried Feodor through his errands at the store, getting him on his horse and out of town as quickly as possible. Jessie's manner irritated him no end, but she stood her ground and refused to answer his questions or even grant him a friendly smile. When Roster was well behind them, she breathed a sigh of relief, brought her horse up to Feodor's, stretched out of her saddle to kiss his cheek.

"I'm sorry," she told him, "I really *had* to get out of there, and there wasn't time to talk about it. An awful lot's been happening, Feodor."

"So I gather," he said shortly. "Jessie, will you please pull up a minute and stop this business?" He reached out for her reins, and Jessie jerked away.

"Just listen, all right? And trust me, Feodor. I don't *want* to stop now."

"Then we won't," he shrugged. "You're not worried about that Lucy Jordan, are you? I doubt she'll hang around here with Ki on her trail."

"No, but Lucy's friends might—and she's got plenty of them around Roster." Jessie hurriedly brought him up to

115

date on the events of the night before, starting with Torgler's involvement with Lucy and Marshal Gaiter, and Gaiter's death in the street later on, in front of both Ki and herself.

"What!" Feodor sat bolt upright in the saddle at the mention of the wolf. "Are you certain, Jessie? The—the creature killed this man in *Roster?*"

"I saw it happen, Feodor."

"And the bullets did not harm the thing," he said tightly.

"No, they didn't, and before you ask me why not, I'll tell you I don't know." She turned on him and held his eyes with hers. "I *do* know that was an honest-to-God American wolf—not some creature out of a Transylvanian fairy tale."

"And your American wolves are immune to bullets, yes?" he said wryly. "This must be a great inconvenience to your farmers and ranchers."

Jessie caught his tone and ignored it.

"I'm not going to tell you I've got all the answers," she said quietly. "But I've sure got a few you don't know about. Which makes it a lot easier for me to understand what's happening here. There's more to all this than I've told you, Feodor."

"Yes, I'm well aware of that," he said without looking at her.

"Please don't be angry, now. I've got my reasons." She hesitated, then went on. Choosing her words carefully, she told him about the European cartel that was her enemy, the organization's awesome power, and their goals in America.

"It's not just your wheatfields they're after," she said. "Multiply that by a hundred, a *thousand* different villages throughout the Midwest. What it adds up to is millions of acres of wheat, Feodor. And control of that wheat means control over people. That's sort of frightening, having that kind of power over lots of hungry folks. The ground we're standing on right now couldn't be worth more if it was solid gold. There've been some pretty bad harvests in Europe, you know. Right now, I guess we're the world's breadbasket, with a lot of people depending on us, and it could stay that way for a long time."

Feodor looked grimly thoughtful. "That is not a good thing, Jessica. I have seen men kill for a loaf of bread."

Jessie nodded. "It could come to that again, too. The cartel could make it happen, use hunger like a weapon. They would, believe me, if it served their purpose. And wheat's just part of the picture, just one of the things they're after. They mean to strangle this country by controlling its railroads, its industry, the government itself—"

"—and the men who run these things," Feodor added quickly. "All this is true, Jessica? There are people with such power?"

Jessie didn't have to answer. He could see by the look in her eyes that the things she'd told him were true.

"And this Torgler is behind it?"

"Part of it. A very small part. Here in Roster, and maybe in other sections of the wheat belt."

"He is not the man Marshal Gaiter told Gustolf about. The man who wants to buy our land."

"Whoever that was, he's one of Torgler's people. Torgler will take over now. He's got your folks stirred up with this werewolf business. Ready to get out at any price." She caught Feodor's look and shook her head. "I don't know how he's doing it. But he *is*. You can believe that, friend . . ."

Ki had no trouble at all following Lucy Jordan's trail. The girl was running her mount hard, moving fast over the prairie and cutting a swath through the knee-high grass as straight and clear as an arrow. At first he thought she'd simply panic and kill her horse and make his job easy. Soon, however, he saw that she'd slowed to an easy gait. Ki nodded and almost smiled. In a way, anything else would have been a disappointment. Lucy Jordan wasn't a lady who was used to losing her head. He had nothing but contempt for what she was, but he had to admire her skill. She'd outfoxed him good back in Roster—twice, as a matter of fact. She was clever and cunning and could think on her feet. You didn't have to like your enemies, but it was foolish to underestimate them. He wouldn't make that mistake again with Lucy Jordan.

Ki reined in his horse at the top of the hill, and let his gaze sweep over the land ahead. It was poor country to run in, a bad place to throw off pursuers. Every way you turned was exactly like the place you'd just been. There were no twisting gullies or canyons for hundreds of miles, only the gently rolling prairie that seemed to stretch out forever.

Ki thought about that. Lucy Jordan knew what she was facing as well as he did. She knew who was after her, too, and that he'd stay on her tail till he got her. Knowing what she did, what was she likely to do next? She sure as hell wouldn't quit—he was dead certain of that. And if she was half as smart as he thought she was...

Ki stopped and came suddenly alert. *That* was the thing that had been plaguing the edge of his mind. Lucy Jordan was running flat out, making no effort to cut left or right, or make a broad circle and slip through behind him. It was the only thing you *could* do on the prairie, and Lucy hadn't even considered it. Why? Ki asked himself. What else did she have in mind? He knew the answer just as well as he knew his name. It was exactly what he'd do himself. They were much alike in that respect, foxes instead of hares. She'd run so far, then turn around and fight. He was certain she'd already made that decision. Now they were both hunters, and both the hunted. Ki, though, figured he was still a few steps ahead. He knew what the girl had in mind, and he had a few tricks up his sleeve that she'd likely never heard of.

He looked at the line of trees a long moment before he realized what he was seeing. The trees hid the creek that wound its way past Gustolf's settlement. He'd circled out of town in an unfamiliar direction, and come in on the other side. Stopping to get his bearings, he guessed the settlement was a good ten miles back to the right.

Ki slid off his horse and studied the ground. Lucy's tracks went off ahead, paralleling the creek, but showing no sign of going near it. Not yet, anyway. He climbed back in the saddle, rode another hundred yards, and stopped abruptly. There—just as he'd figured. Ki grinned and followed the trail with his eyes until it disappeared in high grass, then he extended the path farther in his mind. Lucy had suddenly veered straight for the creek. If he followed her trail and she was waiting for him, he'd be dead in a few minutes. From the cover of the trees, she could see him coming forever—and he already knew she could handle a gun.

Of course, Lucy knew he wouldn't do that, ride straight into a trap. He'd follow the land a good mile or so, then head down the creek himself, cross it, come in behind her, and catch her flat.

Like hell, thought Ki. She isn't anywhere near that creek, not anymore. She's already been down and come back, and she's waiting for me right up ahead. He was sure he was right, but he wouldn't bet his life on it. He'd underestimated Lucy Jordan once before. If *she'd* guessed that *he'd* figure what she might do... Ki tossed that thought aside. It was like the intricate little ivory balls they carved in Japan, one inside the other, and then another and another. You could worry about it forever, and end up doing nothing. He might be wrong, but he wouldn't go near the creek to find out. Instead, he mounted up again and kicked his horse into a run, making a long half-circle over the land. There was always the chance she might break through and pass him, but Ki didn't think so. Lucy was a professional assassin. She'd wait, and rid herself of him once and for all.

When he saw the place, he knew he was right. He'd left the horse in a hollow between the hills and bellied through the tall grass for the last quarter-mile. It looked like an old way station for a stage line, and very likely was. There was a burned-out stone building and the remains of a horse corral. Ki figured it had been there since before Roster was settled.

He crawled up as close as he dared, within thirty yards

119

of the place. After a few moments he knew she wasn't there. The place was too small, too obvious. The only real cover was the shell of the building itself. He'd be foolish to ride into that. What she'd done was take cover in high grass, just as he'd done himself. She was waiting out there, past the abandoned station but somewhere in sight of it. A rider would come up on the place, see right off that it was a good place for an ambush, leave his horse, and come in on foot from behind. And that was when Lucy would get him. Walking, without any cover.

Ki came to his haunches and moved swiftly through the grass at a crouch. He had a good idea where she was. It was the spot he'd pick himself—a clump of grass that appeared innocent enough, but commanded a slightly higher approach to the abandoned building. He stopped, took off his Stetson, and raised his head carefully out of the grass. He couldn't see her, but knew she was there. He could almost sense her presence, see her in his mind's eye. Crawling a few yards farther, he found a slight depression in the land and followed it toward Lucy's position. He stopped again, listened. Nothing. Not even the dry chatter of insects, or the cry of a crow from the creek. For the first time, Ki began to seriously doubt himself. He *knew* she was there. She *had* to be. Still...

It was an old trick, but certainly worth a try. Backing up along the depression, he came to a spot where a few sticks had been washed down the hill in seasons past. The branches were light, brittle, and bleached as white as bone. He found one three feet long with a stubby fork on the end. Digging in his jacket for a length of light string, he attached the cord three-quarters of the way up the stick and carried it quietly back the way he'd come. He laid the stick flat on the ground with the forked end toward him, and dug the fork slightly into the ground. Then he lifted the stick a few inches and placed his Stetson on the other end and backed off, carefully unwinding the cord behind him.

Finally he was a good twenty feet from the hat and the

stick. Listening again, he slowly pulled the string. The stick came up at an angle, and the Stetson peeked over the grass.

Nothing.

Lucy wasn't even tempted. Ki grinned and silently saluted her intelligence. Shooting at a raised hat was foolish. Ki lowered the hat and backed quickly down the depression. She knew where he was now, and would likely take the bait—circle around and wait for him to move. Which was exactly what *he* was doing, too. Of course, she might stay right where she was and just wait for him, but Ki didn't think she'd risk it. He'd told her with his hat that he knew where she was. It took a great deal of nerve to sit still after that.

Ki worked his way up the hill in silence, senses alert to every move, every sound that came his way. Lucy was playing his game now, whether she knew it or not. His samurai training had prepared him for the encounter in a hundred different ways. She could become as a stone, but he would know she was there. Breath whispered in and out of her lungs, and blood coursed through her veins to the beat of her heart. The wind brought him the sharp tang of her hair, and the subtle smell of her skin.

He knew she had a pistol at least, and possibly another rifle by now. He wasn't concerned about that, and didn't feel threatened by the weapons. A weapon was useless unless you could use it. He would not give Lucy Jordan that chance.

He saw her now with *kime*, the sense that feels an enemy's churning life forces. She was close, just above the draw, no more than five yards away, looking just to his right. Ki picked up a small pebble and tossed it less than a foot behind her. He heard her suck in her breath and roll away, then come up fast on her elbows with the weapon thrust out before her. Ki raised an eyebrow and gave her a silent nod of admiration. The girl was good—no, excellent! Not one person in a thousand could have reacted so swiftly—known instantly that it was a pebble and not a person, and held back pressure on the trigger.

Ki knew exactly where she was. He could have bounced a rock off her back. Still, he was learning more about her every minute, and had more respect for her than that. Lucy knew what he was up to and where the pebble had come from. This time she would squeeze off a shot, and in the proper direction, at that. She was good, and she could kill him.

Ki changed his tactics. He threw several more stones high in the air, with very little angle, making a small circle around her, but never too close. It would unnerve her, keep her on edge, but provide nothing to give him away. Finally he tossed five pebbles at once. They settled in the grass only inches from Lucy's head. The sudden assault was too much. Lucy fired three quick shots into the grass.

Ki moved swiftly under cover of the noise, then went to ground again. Once more, Lucy Jordan did the unexpected. Instead of keeping her cover, she sprang up abruptly, legs bent in a crouch, sweeping the weapon before her in a deadly half-circle. Ki came up in a blur. As Lucy jerked around to catch him, he brought his knees up to his chin in midair, turned his body parallel to the ground, and lashed out stiffly with his left foot. The pistol exploded, spitting fire along the plane of his calf and thigh. Lucy's head snapped back and she dropped like a sack.

Ki found the pistol and stuck it in his belt, then lifted the girl's limp form and carried her through the grass toward the abandoned station. She was surprisingly light in his arms. Her head fell loosely over the hollow of his shoulder, baring the creamy white flesh of her throat. Flame-red hair brushed his arm.

"You do not look like an assassin now," he said wondrously. "You look like a woman asleep in my arms." Watching her, it saddened him greatly that she was not at all what she seemed...

★

Chapter 13

A razor-sharp line of shade angled across the dirt floor of the roofless building. Ki squatted on his heels against the wall and watched the girl. She moaned, frowned, and bit her lip, then finally opened her eyes.

"Damn, mister—what'd you *hit* me with, anyway?" She dragged herself to a sitting position and gingerly touched her jaw. "I got a bruise there? Jesus! I think you broke something sure!"

"Nothing is broken," Ki assured her. "You have a small swelling, but it is not serious."

Lucy gave him a narrow look. "Not for you, friend."

"Lucy..." Ki let out a breath and folded his hands on his legs. "I know exactly how badly you are bruised, because I *know* how hard I hit you. A little harder and you'd have a fractured jaw. Harder than that and I would have snapped your neck. Then you would not be sitting there complaining."

Lucy closed one eye. "You mean that, don't you?"

"Yes, I most certainly do."

"You're pretty good at that stuff, aren't you? I'd sure like to learn some of those moves, whatever it is you call 'em."

Ki looked pained. "You're not going to *need* any more tricks, Lucy."

"Oh, yeah, I keep forgettin'." She stuck out her lower lip in a pout. "You're going to take me back, right?"

"Yes, of course I am."

"Or *try*, anyway." She shot him a quick wink, blue eyes flashing with such a challenge Ki had to laugh in amazement.

"That doesn't mean a thing to you, does it? You're not even twenty-five, and you'll likely spend the rest of your life in prison, but—"

"Shit, mister—" She thrust out her chin and gave him a bold, penetrating look. "Talkin' about it and bein' there are two different things. Right?"

"*No,*" Ki said flatly. He came to his feet and jabbed a finger in her direction. "In this case they are the same, Lucy. And the sooner you understand that, the sooner we can talk."

"Jesus Christ—talk about what?"

"Going to prison for life, or going for only a short time." He paused and looked down at her. "Or possibly—not going at all. Though I don't think that's too likely."

"Oh!" Lucy threw back her head and laughed. "Here it comes at last. If I'm a real good girl, you'll put in a word for me with Jessica Starbuck herself. She'll pull some strings with the President or someone and I get off real easy." Lucy's eyes went hard. "Not on your goddamn life, mister."

"Not even on *yours*, Lucy? It really doesn't matter?"

"No, why should it?"

Ki almost believed her, but the faint spot of white at the corner of her mouth, the tight cords in her throat told him a different story. Lucy Jordan lied well with her eyes, but the rest of her body gave her away. Ki walked a few steps and put his hands in his pockets. "It's up to you, of course. I'm not sure Jessie will help, even if you give the right answers. She isn't too pleased with you."

Lucy grinned at that and came to her feet, brushing the dirt off her denims. "Trouble is, friend, I don't *know* anything, though I don't reckon you an' Miss Starbuck'd believe that, would you?"

"You know who hired you."

"Right. And so do you. It was Torgler. Now what the hell's *that* worth?"

"Nothing. Not by itself. But you've been around the man, heard him talk about his operation, the people he works for."

"Torgler? Are you serious?" Lucy made a face. "That man's slick as a snake. He don't tell *any*body more'n they need to know."

"You know about the wolves, Lucy. How does he work that? Who's in on it with him?"

"Hey, hold it now!" Lucy's eyes got wide and she shook her head firmly. "I don't know nothin' about that stuff, and I don't *want* to, either."

Ki's eyes bored into her. "You expect me to believe that?"

"Believe whatever you want!" she said hotly, clenching her fists at her sides. "I was hired to get rid of Jessica Starbuck. Hell, there's no use lyin' about that. They want her out of the way, and they want her real bad. Torgler's got orders from someone a lot higher up on the ladder than he is, I know that much."

"But you don't know who?"

"No, of course not."

"You're sure?"

"*Yes,* I'm *sure!*" Lucy stopped and ran a hand over her face. "Look, you know more about this setup than *I* do. It's big—real big. I'm hired help and that's all. High-priced help, maybe, but so what? All that does is get you a bigger wad of bills. It sure don't entitle you to know who's on the other end of it. In my business, that's not real healthy information to have."

"Is that what you call it?" Ki asked evenly. "A business?"

Lucy gave him a nasty grin. "We going to talk 'bout that now? How'd a sweet little thing like me get in the killin' trade?" She waved him off and handed him a sigh. "You mind tossin' me that canteen? I could sure use a drink, but I expect all you got there's water."

"Yes, that's all."

"Hell, I'll take what I can get."

Ki picked up the canteen and tossed it to her by the strap. Lucy grabbed for it and missed, bent quickly to retrieve it, whirled about on her knees, and scooped a handful of dirt in Ki's face. Ki saw it coming, threw an arm in front of his eyes, and twisted aside as the canteen came at him from Lucy's other hand. She held it by the strap and whipped it at his head like a missile. Ki knocked it aside, grabbed Lucy's waist, and twisted her off her feet. Lucy yelled, clawed empty air, and hit the ground hard. Ki came down on top of her and slammed her wrists into the dirt. The girl squirmed to get her legs free and kick him, but Ki's whole weight was upon her.

"God *damn* you!" Lucy glared at him from under a tangled veil of hair. "I shoulda killed you back in Roster. I'd be long gone from this place if I had!"

"It's not because you didn't try," sighed Ki. "Are you finished now? Can we stop this?"

"Just can't stand it, huh?"

"What do you mean?"

Her lips curled in a sneer. "Bein' on top of a girl bother you all that much?"

Ki stared at her and laughed. "The town's way back there, Lucy. Yelling rape won't work this time."

"Oh? An' who's callin' for help?" Her eyes flashed with mischief and she bit her lip in a grin. "Maybe if I just—struggled a little harder I could—*mmmmm*, yeah!" She

126

looked right at him and ground her hips against him in a slow, undulating circle. "Am I—gettin' any closer to escaping? *Feels* like I might be making some progress..."

Ki had to smile at her teasing. "I don't think you're escaping, Lucy, But you *are* making some progress."

"Oh? Well, that's nice..."

It *was* nice, Ki had to admit. She knew just what to do and where to do it. The hard press of her pelvis searched him out, and his member grew steadily under her touch.

"Say, now..." Lucy's eyes sparkled with pleasure. *"Do* have some feelings, don't you? Kinda wondered about you..."

"Oh? And why was that?"

"I don't know, I just—oh, *yes!*" Ki thrust himself against her and she opened her eyes wide. "Can't...really remember at the moment...not when you do things like that..." Her mouth opened and her face flushed with color. Ki watched a vein throb in the long column of her neck. Her breath came in rapid little bursts, and her breasts stretched the worn fabric of her shirt.

Lucy caught his glance and mocked him with her eyes. "If you like that, why don't you unbutton my shirt and get a better look?"

"I was just thinking the very same thing."

"Really? I never would've known."

Ki released her wrists and she clasped them tightly around his shoulders. He ran his fingers quickly along the buttons of her shirt, baring the firm swell of her breasts. He slid the cloth aside and brushed his fingers gently across her nipples. Lucy groaned with pleasure at his touch. He stroked the silken nubs and felt them tighten under his fingers, saw them turn from dusty pink to the flush of scarlet.

"Ahhhh!" Lucy trembled and wet her lips. "Kiss them— please!" she begged him. "Now! *Now!*"

"Would you like that?"

"Oh, yes!"

"They are very lovely."

"Are they?"

"Yes. Hard and soft at the same time."

Lucy shut her eyes. "Raise up a little. All right?"

"What?"

"No, don't stop *doing* what you're doing to me. Just—move a little so I can peel out of these damn trousers. Don't think I'm gonna need 'em much longer."

Ki grinned and obliged gladly, and Lucy's hand snaked down over her belly to struggle with her belt. He watched the delicious peaks of her breasts, marveling at the way her pert little nipples continued to grow. He bent to take the sweet nubs of pleasure in his mouth; the musky taste of her womanhood tingled on his lips and assailed his senses. The sharp, exotic flavor of her flesh heightened his excitement and sent a raw surge of heat coursing through his veins.

Lucy squirmed and arched her back, forcing her breasts into his mouth. Her hand worked frantically at her waist, tearing at the tight-fitting denims.

"Are they—good?" she whispered.

"Yes!"

"Nice little tits?"

"Yes, Lucy!"

"Are—mine as nice as hers?" she said breathlessly. "When you put Jessica Starbuck's nipples in your mouth, do they—"

"No!" The words shook him, tore at his gut like a blade. He jerked up on his arms and stared. "That's not true," he blurted. "I never—" Ki caught himself and stopped.

"Oh, my..." The surprise in Lucy's eyes narrowed to understanding. She held his gaze until Ki pushed her roughly away. He quickly got to his feet and turned from her, grinding his teeth to control his anger.

"It's that way, is it?" she said behind him. "You want to, but you haven't. Damn—you can't even think about it, can you? I see, now..."

"Damn it, Lucy!" He turned on her, eyes blazing with a fury that set her aback. "You see *nothing!*"

Lucy raised a brow and shrugged. "Sure. Whatever you say, friend."

"Where is your horse?"

"Huh?"

"I said, where is your *horse!*"

Lucy stuck out her chin in a pout. "You want it, go find it!"

"Fine," muttered Ki, I'll just do that." He prowled across the dirt floor like a cat, searching the ruins with his gaze.

"What you lookin' for?"

"My jacket."

"Why?"

Ki stopped and turned on her. She stood against the far wall, hands on her hips. The stance threw the curve of one thigh into a sharp, provocative angle. She'd made no effort to buckle the denims. They still hung loosely over her hips, baring a patch of creamy flesh across the flat of her belly. The swell of her breasts pushed the open blouse aside, and a tumble of red hair veiled her face.

She looked at him and laughed. "Well, what're you starin' at? Go find the goddamn horse."

"I will," he said tightly. He picked up his jacket where he'd left it on the far side of the room and searched through the pockets. His own Colt, and the one he'd taken from her, were laid neatly in the fold. "Soon as I find some cord to tie you up."

"To what?" Lucy blew hair out of her eyes and grinned uneasily. "Look, you don't have to do that. I'm not *goin'* anywhere."

"Now why don't I believe that?"

Lucy opened her mouth to protest, then let out a breath and squinted at the open sky. "The horse is tied down by the creek," she said wearily.

"Thought it might be."

"And you don't have to tie me up. I can't stand bein' tied. I promise. Please? I'll stay *right* here."

It was Ki's turn to laugh. "Don't be ridiculous, Lucy."

He found a length of cord and started toward her.

"Wait!" She stood up straight and held out a hand. "If I give you all my clothes, I *can't* go running naked around the countryside, now can I?"

"Lucy—"

Before he could stop her, she bent to yank off her boots and strip the tight denims over her legs. Throwing him a bold and saucy grin, she grabbed the open blouse and deliberately ripped it in two pieces and tossed the shreds of cloth at his feet.

Lucy spread her legs, put her hands on her hips, and sighed. "That's the *second* shirt I've torn up today, and I haven't *got* any more pants. So I'm sure not goin' anywhere. I'm 'bout as jaybird-naked as a girl can get."

Ki stared. "Yes. I—see that."

Lucy gave him a wink. "Thought maybe you did." She tossed a riot of flame-red hair over her shoulders and boldly thrust out her breasts. "Besides, friend, I kinda wanted you to see what you're missin'. I'm not all *that* bad, am I? Couldn't we just take up where we left off and forget the damn horses? Honest to God, I didn't mean to say all that stuff, an' it's got nothin' to do with—"

Ki dropped his jacket, took two long strides, and drew her into his arms. Lucy gave a joyous little cry and thrust her lips hungrily up to meet him. Ki kissed her soundly, letting his tongue savor the warm, honey hollows of her mouth. Her fingers busied themselves with his trousers, tearing away at the buckle and the buttons underneath. She knelt to slip the fabric over his hips and down his legs. Her hair brushed his belly and the hardness of his thighs, the soft touch searing his flesh like a brand. Lucy's hands explored his belly, raced like fire along the small of his back, then finally came to rest between his legs. She raised her head then, and met his eyes longingly with her own.

"You gave *me* a real nice kiss," she said in a voice he could barely hear. "Now I think I'll give you one in return. That all right with you?"

"Just as right as it can be, Lucy—"

Bending again, she knelt and leaned back on her legs, reached up and cupped his scrotum gently in her palms, and softly kissed the tip of his member. Ki watched himself swell at her touch, felt the tender shaft go rigid as iron. She pressed two fingers about him and held him up straight while her lips pressed kisses along his length. Ki closed his eyes and let a whisper of pleasure pass through his teeth. She nibbled at him like some small animal timidly inspecting its prize; her tongue flicked out to tease him, stroke him quickly with moisture, then retreat into the warmth of her mouth. Her lips opened around him, not touching him at all, but letting her hot breath caress him.

Ki's whole body went stiff. He yearned for her mouth, ached for the press of her lips. Lucy, though, would come no closer. She denied him her touch, continued to provoke him with the furnace of her breath.

"Good Lord," moaned Ki. "Are you certain you aren't Japanese? I have never—"

She pulled away a moment and gave him a sleepy grin. "You like that?" she said innocently. "Am I doing it right, darling?"

"That depends on what you mean by right. If it's scraping my nerves raw, yes—"

Lucy purred and planted a moist kiss on the head of his shaft. "I *sure* wouldn't want to make you nervous..."

"Uh, no." Ki nearly jumped out of his skin. "I can see that you wouldn't."

"Thought I was Japanese, huh?"

"Yes...the exquisite tortures of love are a practiced art in that country. The—*Lucy!*" Ki gasped. He felt as if he'd suddenly been swallowed in satin. At first he thought she'd pressed her mouth around him, then stared down over the flat plane of his belly to see this wasn't so. Lucy had made a nest out of her long red tresses. The hair was piled loosely in the palm of her hand, her fingers clasped about his rigid member. Ki groaned as she stroked him back and forth with

131

the fiery tumble of hair. The feeling was almost unbearable, an agony of pleasure that tightened every cord and tendon in his body, and engorged his shaft with blood until he thought it would surely explode.

"Lucy... Lucy... I'm—"

"Oh, no you're not," Lucy said softly, "you just *think* you are..."

The pressure in his loins swelled to bursting, hung for a long moment on the joyous edge of relief, then slid back with a sigh.

"My *God*, woman!" Ki's body was wet with perspiration, every nerve twisted and screaming for release. "Lucy—I can't stay where you have taken me. I've got to go one way or the other."

Lucy brushed hair out of her eyes, stretched up, and pressed her cheek in the hollow of his thighs. "Just where is it you'd like to go, dear?"

"*Anywhere*," Ki said. "Please!"

"You are not being very Japanese," she reminded him.

"Lucy, I'm only *half* Japanese. That half is thoroughly enjoying the exquisite torture of hanging on the edge of a cliff. The American half is about to go crazy!"

Lucy bit her lip and gave him a mischievous grin. "Well, we'll see what we can do. For *both* halves, huh?" She took his throbbing shaft between her fingers and stroked it lightly with her tongue, again and again, like a kitten lapping up cream. Suddenly the strokes became harder, faster, until the pink tip of her tongue darted over him like a snake. She opened her mouth to encircle him. Lucy slid her arms around his waist, and dug her nails into the hard flesh of his hips.

He felt the storm churning up within him, thundering up through his loins. It tingled over his flesh, rushed into his member until he could contain the pleasure no longer.

Lucy groaned and writhed against him, straining to take him within her. Her cheeks went hollow with her hunger, and the explosion burst inside him, coursed between them, and filled her mouth with his warmth. Lucy trembled all over, and eagerly drank in the joy she'd created...

★

Chapter 14

She lay back quietly in his arms, eyes half closed under a
heavy veil of lashes. Ki watched her, letting his eyes feast
on the lazy stretch of her legs, the delicious swell of her
thighs. He followed the lines of her body, pausing a moment
at the soft nest of amber-tinted fur, moving past the hollow
of her belly to the proud curve of her breasts.

Lucy moaned and moved against him, drawing her knees
up under her chin, nestling the ivory length of her legs
between his own. She was a small, sleek little creature, a
cat curling up for its afternoon nap. An errant beam of
sunlight slanted through the ruined stone walls and painted
a tawny stripe across her bottom. There was a small bruise
on the side of her hip, the skin hardly broken. It was the
spot where his *sai* had grazed her on the rooftops of Roster.
Ki shook his head. Clearly, the weapon had scared her more
then anything else. Now he was glad this was so. He grinned
and ran a finger over the plushly rounded flesh, following
the curves into shadow and the soft touch of down.

Lucy shuddered and opened one eye. "Mmmmmm, now
that's very nice."

"Good. Why don't you wake up and enjoy it? *I'm* the one who ought to be sleepy, Lucy. After what you did to me."

"Oh? And what was that? Can't hardly remember."

"Hah!" Ki slapped her lightly across the hips. "You took absolutely everything out of me, that's what."

"Yeah, I did, didn't I?" She gave him a small sigh and wet her lips. "Absolutely *every*thing."

"Well . . . not everything."

She blinked and raised a skeptical brow. "I know what you're thinking, and you don't have to at all, friend. I got some awful good feelings givin' you pleasure, and I don't need a thing. All right?"

"All right," Ki said solemnly. "It's nice to know you are a fully satisfied woman."

"Well, I am. Really."

"Yes. That's fine," he said, lazily trailing a finger into the cleft between her hips. The finger touched a silky line of down, then slipped further to brush the moist folds of her pleasure.

Lucy jerked and made a little noise at his touch. "Hey— what are you doin' down there?"

"Nothing that would greatly interest you."

"You don't think so?"

"Of course not. You have no further needs, remember?"

"*All* right, now . . ."

"Pay no attention to me. Pretend I'm not here."

"That's—not real easy to do . . ."

"Of course it is. You are a master of prolonging a man's pleasure. I'm sure you can do as well when you're on the other end."

Lucy shuddered again. "Only thing is, that—*other end* you're playing with is attached to me. Oh, Gawd, mister!" Ki lightly slipped his finger into her wetness, and the girl nearly jumped out of her skin.

"You are a *very* sensitive woman. Did you know that?"

134

"Did I *know* that?" Lucy sucked in a breath and came to her knees. "Of course I know that! How can I help it?" She started to move off her knees, but Ki rested a firm hand on her shoulders and held her back.

"Now what's that for, friend?" Her eyes were dark and smoldering, and he knew the question was no question at all.

"Just stay right there. I'll show you." He let his hand slide down the delicious curve of her back and come to rest on her bottom. He kept his hand there, rubbing his palm in a slow, circular motion. Lucy responded instantly, arching her back and twisting under his touch. Slowly her knees slid over the ground, stretching her legs apart as her shoulders sank to cradle her head in her arms. Ki felt himself swell with desire at the delightful sight before him. The long, tapered columns of her legs thrust her bottom high in the air, opening her sweet treasures to his touch.

"Is that what you wanted?" she purred. "Got everything you like now?"

"Yes," Ki said hoarsely. "Everything is here, I am certain of that." The sleepy, satisfied look in her eyes told him she relished his gaze on her body; opening herself to him gave her pleasure and heightened her own excitement.

"So now that you got it, what you figure on doin' with it?"

"Several ideas have come to me."

"Such as?" she taunted. "Tell me!"

Ki didn't answer. Instead, he moved up behind her on his knees and grasped the firm globes of her bottom in his hands. Lucy moaned softly as he stretched her flesh with his palms, then lightly brushed her hips with his belly.

She knew what was coming, and her slender form trembled in anticipation. His fingers moved down to part the soft, fleshy petals between her thighs. Even before he reached her, the promise of his touch triggered a surge of hot juices.

135

"Please, please, oh, *yes!*" she whispered.

"What? You would accept more pleasure than you have been given?"

"Oh, stop that! I mean—no, *don't!*"

"This surprises me greatly," said Ki. "I am totally confused now." He tried hard to keep the laughter out of his voice, but Lucy's cute little bottom twitching before him made it an almost impossible task.

"Please," Lucy moaned, "don't—play games with me. I can't—stand it!"

"Well. Perhaps a *small* amount of pleasure..."

"I don't *want* anything small!" wailed Lucy.

The musky nest glistened before him like a pink treasure of jewels. Ki brought his rigid member close, kissed her flesh lightly with the tip, and pulled away. Lucy jerked back, trying desperately to find him. "Where *are* you, damn it!"

"Right here," said Ki. "Not far."

"Far enough," she snapped irritably. "Look, I can't— ahhhhh!"

Ki teased her with another light touch, and then another, slightly deeper. "Lucy—don't *move,* now. All right? Stay exactly where you are. Perfectly still."

"I—don't think I can."

"You can if you try." He entered her again, slowly, holding her waist tightly with his hands while his member slid into her warmth, all the way to the bottom. He stayed there a long moment, not moving at all, then drew himself out.

"Ohhh!" Lucy sighed and almost collapsed. "I never felt *any*thing like that before!"

"Good," said Ki. "We'll do it again sometime."

"You bastard," Lucy cried, "don't even *say* that! Please," she begged, "get back inside me, huh? I'll be still. I'll be *per*fectly still..."

"Good. That's the art of it, Lucy. Being almost there,

136

then refraining from anything more. You already know that, as you have demonstrated on me."

"Yeah, well, that's—different."

"No. There is no difference at all. Except, as you put it so well, now you're on the other end."

Lucy laughed in spite of herself. Ki thrust himself gently into the sweet honey-warmth between her thighs, grasped her waist, and slid his length up to the hilt. Lucy gave a strangled little cry, but didn't move. He rocked on his knees, drawing her to him, then moving her away. Lucy caught the gentle motion and joined it.

He grinned at the curve of her back, knowing what she was up to. She was playing his rules to the letter, and boldly cheating at the same time. As he slid in and out of her charms, she tightened subtly around him, stroking him with moist caresses. She was challenging his game with her own, and it was a hard one to beat. The deeper and slower he thrust himself inside her, the more chance he gave her to practice her art. The trick was taking its toll, pushing him toward the edge a great deal faster than he'd intended. He slowed his pace, which delighted Lucy to no end; instead of solving his problem, he merely compounded it. The action gave her even *more* time to bring her tender vise into play.

"You—know what you are doing, don't you?" moaned Ki. "If you—would only—cooperate . . ."

"Doing?" Lucy said blandly. "Who's doing what?"

"Lucy, I'm *in* there. I know exactly what you're doing."

"Whatever it is, I'm certain it can't affect your—*lovely* Oriental discipline."

Ki groaned and laughed. She stroked him gently with soft, velvety muscles, kneading him ever closer, swelling him to the exquisite edge of his release. He was determined to hold her off, but the girl had incredible control of those warm silken walls. In another few seconds, another stroke or two . . .

Ki closed his eyes and let out a deep breath, trying desperately to slow the thing welling up within him. His heart pounded frantically in his chest, surging blood through his veins. He relaxed, slowly, consciously withdrawing the feeling from his body. He was still there, thrusting himself inside her, but a part of him was somewhere else. He gripped Lucy hard, squeezing the slender circle of her waist, plunging his shaft again and again to the heart of her pleasure. Lucy squealed and tried to tear herself from his grip. The tables were suddenly turned. She gave a little cry and writhed against him. He lifted her into a deep, swelling orgasm that wrenched her with pain and pleasure. She hung there a moment, trembling on the crest, then fell back drained and exhausted. Her long legs collapsed, but Ki held on. He thrust himself deeper, drawing her naked thighs about his waist. Lucy lay limp on her belly, nails clawing the ground. Her back was sleek and wet, dotted with tiny pearls of moisture.

She begged him to stop, her voice a ragged slur without words. Ki carried her up to the heights again and again, until one delicious orgasm flowed into the next. Her body went rigid, curved into a bow—and at that precise moment, Ki let himself feel once more. His loins exploded with a violence that loosed a terrible cry from his lungs. He pumped her with liquid heat, filled her belly with fire. Lucy joined his joyous cry. His orgasm merged with her own and tossed them both into a syrupy whirlpool of pleasure . . .

"It doesn't matter, does it?" she whispered into his shoulder. "What you are or what I am or anything . . ."

"Hush." He stroked her red hair and pulled her to him. "There is no need to talk."

"There is, though, isn't there?" She leaned up on his chest and he saw the pain and sadness behind her gaze. This was not the Lucy Jordan he had known. The thing they'd shared had stripped her of a great deal more than her clothing. Now the ice-blue windows of her eyes were open to something she'd seldom let herself see, and she was frightened of what was there.

"When we leave here, we won't be the same people who made that lovin'," she said tightly. "We'll—be what we were."

"People are never what they were. They change. They do not have to be the same."

"We—" She looked at him, bit her lip, and lowered her eyes. "You think—we could be different?" He started to answer, but her words rushed out to stop him. "I don't mean you'd have to stay with me or anything, but we could try. We could start out and see. Maybe something would work. If we go back there—" She stopped suddenly, and let out a sigh.

"Lucy..."

"No. You don't have to say it." She gave a brittle little laugh. "Jesus—I gotta be crazy to talk like that. You an' me would have about as much chance as—what? What is it?" She gave him a curious look, and Ki shook his head.

"I don't know. Stay here. It's probably nothing." He came to his feet, padded naked across the floor to the blackened stone wall, and picked up his Colt. Afternoon shadows were stretched across the flats, and the earth shimmered up to the sky in waves of heat. The ground dipped just past the ruined way station toward the low line of trees along the creek. He could just see the gray-green crown of foliage from where he stood. He walked around the wall, keeping to cover as best he could, letting his senses roam the bright horizon. Nothing. Lucy caught his eye and he shook his head. If anything had been there, it was gone now. Still...

Ki turned away and saw it out of the corner of his eye. Something moved. In the high grass near the front of the station, where he and Lucy had tracked one another hours before. He motioned the girl to stay where she was, and before she could speak he was gone, moving low and fast into the open.

He stopped, listened, moved forward again—then froze

139

in his tracks. The sound chilled his blood and wrenched his gut with fear. He turned on his heels and ran, knowing he'd never make it. The grass tore apart and the thing came at him, an ugly growl rising in its throat.

"Lucy, get out!" he shouted.

Ki dug his feet into the earth and twisted away. The wolf sprang past him, slamming him to the ground and tearing the Colt from his grip. Suddenly, Lucy came out of shadow, her naked form startlingly pale in the harsh light. In one motion she scrambled across the dirt floor for his jacket, scooped her pistol out of the folds, and whipped it toward the charging animal.

White fire exploded. Lucy screamed and went down, her terrible cry raking every nerve in Ki's body. He rolled to his feet and stared. The thing ripped and tore, spattered creamy skin with flecks of crimson, staggered on its feet, then collapsed across her breasts.

"Luuuuuuucy!" Bile rose in his throat. He ran to her, face twisted in pain. Trembling with anger and rage, he lifted the beast from her body and threw it against the wall.

"No, damn it, *no!*" he shouted hoarsely. "You can't be, I won't *let* you—"

A bullet ripped flesh along his thigh. Another hit stone and whined away. Ki jerked back, clawing for cover as the sound of the shots rolled over the plains.

Ki's mind raced. He tried to keep his eyes off Lucy's small figure, fought to quell the anger that boiled in his blood. It was happening again, just as before. The hunter had him trapped, stuck in a hole like a hare. Only this time was different. This time, Ki knew the hunter. And this time, Zascha was not playing a game. He had no intention of letting him go.

Ki, however, had no intention of staying. He would not make the same mistake twice—wait until the hunter could make him guess his new position. The pistol was lying between Lucy and the animal, gleaming in the sun. He didn't even think about trying for it. Zascha would be waiting for that. Instead, he moved along the wall, slipped on his pants, and retrieved his jacket. The Stetson was too exposed and he left it. Stretching every muscle in his body, he braced himself, leaped for the top of the broken wall, grasped hard stone, and threw himself over. Three shots rang out behind him, stitching a path in the dirt. But Ki was already lost in the high grasses...

He had no idea whether Zascha would guess what he'd do, and he didn't much care. In a way, he hoped the man knew he was after him, stalking him under the trees on the quiet banks of the creek. He stopped only long enough to wash out the wound where the charging animal had grazed his shoulder. The place where Zascha's bullet had creased his thigh was only an angry cut and didn't concern him.

Lucy was never far from his mind. He no longer tried to put her image aside. He steeled himself to look at it, the way she was in life, her naked arms about him, eyes flashing her love. And the way she was in death. He held up the picture and made himself see it.

A dozen questions raced through his head. He had no answers for any of them. Had Lucy chosen the old way station for a purpose? Ki wondered. At first he'd assumed she stopped there deliberately to make a stand. She knew he was on her trail, and it was a convenient place for an ambush. Now, since Zascha and the wolf had found them there, he wasn't all that sure. Maybe Torgler had *told* her to go there. Ki knew for certain she thought she could trick him and get away. Maybe even kill him. The handful of sand and the canteen had proven that.

The thought came up and touched him, whether he wanted to see it or not. Lucy's passion was real, but hadn't started out that way at all. Maybe it had *never* been real. Maybe—hell, if she could have gotten the pistol before... Ki cast the thought aside. It hadn't been that way at all, damn it. She'd killed the wolf and saved him...

And who was the animal after? he asked himself silently. Lucy, or himself? Torgler had silenced Gaiter. Why not Lucy as well? After she'd failed to kill Jessie in Roster, she was little more use to the man...

It was another question he might as well forget. No one was likely to give him the answer.

Zascha was making no effort to cover his trail. A few hundred yards down the creek, Ki saw where the man had led both Ki's horse and Lucy's across the water, gotten quickly on another mount, and torn through the trees with the two animals in tow.

Ki stopped and frowned thoughtfully into the woods. Clearly, Zascha was in one hell of a hurry. Why? Why was he making tracks when he really didn't have to? Even if he knew Ki might follow, that wouldn't bother him at all. He was a skilled hunter and marksman. If anything, sticking around to finish off his foe would have been a wise move. Ki had counted on the possibility and taken great care in his pursuit. Zascha, though, hadn't waited around for a minute.

Ki dropped all caution and bolted through the woods, following the clear tracks of the three horses. Something was wrong. Very wrong. He could feel it, sense it in the air. It was right there, taunting him, just out of sight...

Ki decided it was four o'clock, maybe a little after. There was still plenty of light—the midsummer sun wouldn't set till eight or eight-thirty. He'd have no trouble making it back to the village. And Zascha, of course, wouldn't have the nerve to show up there again. He was convinced, now, that the man was playing a far more important role in Torgler's plan that he'd first imagined. He was more than just a troublemaker, a paid informer in Gustolf's settlement. He was almost certain to be the keeper of the wolves, the man who—

142

Ki stopped, letting his eyes sweep the soft ground ahead. The trail had suddenly changed. The running horses had passed this way, but—there was something else.there, too.

He bent to the ground a moment, then jerked to his feet and stared. *Wolf tracks!* And more than one animal, too. They'd been here, right where he was standing, and not too long ago.

That was startling enough, but there was more to it than that. Something that raised the hackles on his neck and brought the stink of his own fear to his nostrils. Mingled among the tracks was another, more chilling set of prints. Ki set his own foot inside one of the things and quickly pulled it away. God! It was twice, nearly three times as big as his own! What the hell kind of a man made a track like that!

Now, at least, he had some idea why Zascha was in such a great hurry to leave...

★

Chapter 15

It took all the restraint Jessie could muster to keep from showing her frustration and anger. Feodor carefully explained to Gustolf everything that had happened in Roster—relying on Jessie to fill in the gaps. She told him about the cartel, how they'd hired Lucy Jordan to kill her, and how she'd almost gotten away with it on the train—then tried again in town. She explained Torgler's role, how he'd used Marshal Gaiter, and then had him murdered. Gustolf listened politely, but Jessie knew he didn't believe a word of what she was saying. As soon as he learned the wolf had struck again, he cast everything she'd told him aside.

"You see?" The color drained from his features and he shook a trembling hand in her face. "It has happened—just as I knew it would! The curse is upon us. It has taken our people, and now an outsider as well!"

"Father, please." Sonia tried to keep him down, but Gustolf pushed her off and struggled to his feet. He seemed terribly weak to Jessie—much more so than the day before. She wondered if it was the wounds he'd received, or his own fear that was draining his strength. More likely the latter, she decided. He *believed* he was tainted by the wolf, that he'd soon become one of the creatures himself. He was a strong, tough old man, Jessie knew. But not as strong as the fears that tugged at his heart.

"I know what you think," Jessie told him. "There *is* a wolf out there and it's killing people. But there's nothing mystical about it. Believe me. I know these people. They're using your own superstition to frighten you into selling. This is Torgler's doing, and nothing else!"

Gustolf gave her a cold, disparaging look. "You mean well, lady. I know this. But you are not one of us."

"Neither was the marshal," snapped Jessie. "How come the man-wolf got *him?*"

"There are things not so easily understood as you might think, Miss Starbuck."

"Yes," Jessie fumed, "I'm beginning to understand that."

"Jessica—" Feodor frowned in warning.

"Huh-uh. Don't, Feodor." She got up and started across the room. "I think maybe you're right and I'm wrong. There isn't any use in fighting this thing. You and your people won't change. I don't think they can. I—" Jessie stopped in her tracks, stared out the window a moment, then tossed back her hair and laughed out loud. "Would you like to see someone who speaks with *reason,* Gustolf? Well, you've got your wish, my friend."

"What?" Gustolf blinked. "What are you saying?"

"We were just talking about him, remember?" Jessie nodded out the window. "Torgler. And right on schedule, at that. Must've left right in our tracks, Feodor." She turned a rueful eye on Gustolf. "Bet he's brought you the money for your land, too. He knows you're running scared."

"By *God!*" Gustolf shook all over. "You cannot say these things to me!"

"You're right," said Jessie. "This isn't my business anymore." Her green eyes touched him a moment, then she turned and walked out the door and marched straight past Torgler.

Torgler turned on his horse and looked at her, a slight hint of amusement in his ice-blue eyes. He didn't seem at all surprised to see her. "Miss Starbuck. A pleasure as always."

"Speak for yourself," Jessie muttered without looking up. She stopped on the common, a little apart from the others. The immigrants seemed to know what was about, and were already gathering at Gustolf's cottage. The old man limped out, clutching his silver-headed cane, Sonia at his side. Torgler climbed off his horse and walked toward the cottage. He was resplendent as always, Jessie noted sourly. Today he was dressed in a brown riding suit with Stetson to match. A green silk ascot peeked out of a cream-colored shirt, and his knee-length riding boots were clearly expensive and handmade. He knows exactly what he looks like to these people, thought Jessie. He could easily be the haughty count coming down from the manor to see his serfs. The whole thing was deliberate, and it made Jessie's blood boil.

Torgler mumbled something Jessie couldn't hear, and shook hands with Gustolf. She was determined to keep her mouth shut, but she couldn't help moving a few steps closer. Gustolf was squinting carefully at a paper Torgler had pulled out of his coat. He read it silently for a long moment, then a furrow creased his brow.

"These—these numbers are not right," he protested. "The other man, the one in town, he offered us more."

Torgler took back the paper and smiled. "That was Mr. Watson, sir. One of my employees. The money he offered per acre was in line with the market at the time. *These* prices reflect today's needs. Things change very quickly." He shrugged. "Times are hard, and land prices are down, sir."

"Oh, for God's sake!" Jessie couldn't keep quiet. "Times aren't bad. They're booming, Torgler, and you know it." She shook her head at Gustolf. "Land prices are *up*, not down!"

"You are not exactly a disinterested party here, are you, miss?" Torgler said evenly. The crowd muttered agreement.

"Keep out of this," warned Gustolf. "He—he is right. You do not wish us to sell the land. We all know that."

"No." Jessie shook her head and jammed her thumbs in her belt. "You're wrong. I didn't, but I don't feel that way anymore. I think you ought to take whatever Mr. Torgler here is willing to give you, and move on."

"What?" Gustolf looked aghast. Feodor's expression didn't change, but Torgler's cold eyes narrowed at Jessie. "I'm sorry. I said it before and I meant it. I don't think you belong here," Jessie said softly. "I don't think it's your kind of country. Too many wolves and ghosties running about."

The crowd muttered angrily, but Jessie stood her ground. Gustolf's puzzlement turned suddenly to understanding. "Ah, of course." He looked scornfully at Jessie and stepped out to face his people. "Miss Starbuck is an American. She laughs at what she does not understand. This is easy to do, I think, when it is not your own who are dying." He looked squarely at Torgler. "We sell," he said stubbornly. "We sell now." His eyes swept out in a challenge at the others. "I am the elder here. I say this is to be."

No one spoke, but Jessie saw more than one man look shamefully down at his boots. They had worked hard to get where they were. Throwing it all away wasn't that easy.

"A wise decision," said Torgler. He gave Gustolf an easy smile and handed him back the paper. "I need your signature, sir. I have the money here in cash." Gustolf took the paper, and Jessie's heart sank. Suddenly, Feodor took one step forward, grabbed the paper from the old man, and shoved it back at Torgler.

Torgler stared. Gustolf looked as if Feodor had hit him in the stomach. The crowd muttered in anger and surprise, and several men shouted and shook their fists.

"No," Feodor said flatly. "No, old man. You will sell nothing. Not today."

Gustolf came at him in a fury, swept back his arm, and struck at Feodor's face with the cane. Feodor stopped the blow easily, and jerked the cane from Gustolf's grasp.

148

Gustolf staggered back, unable to believe what was happening.

"Feodor, *no!*" shouted Sonia.

"You do not attack your elder!" growled Gustolf. "Give me the cane. It is not yours to hold!"

"It is," Feodor said calmly, "for I have taken it from you." He looked solemnly at Gustolf, and Jessie could see the pain in his eyes. "I am sorry, Gustolf. I respect you greatly. More than any man I know. But this is a thing I must do. I—" The words stuck in his throat. "I do not think you are fit to make this decision. I think your wounds have weakened you, and you can no longer serve as elder." He looked out and searched the crowd. "I do this because I must, because we cannot lose what we have fought so hard to gain. If there are any who would challenge this, let me hear you now. Is there one among you who would be Keeper of the Silver Cane?"

Again, Feodor searched the faces of his people, and Jessie knew exactly who he was looking for: Zascha. If there was any man there who might stir up the crowd and turn them against him, Zascha would be the one. Yet the burly hunter was nowhere to be seen. Where was he? Jessie wondered. She didn't trust the man at all, and knew Ki had reason to like him even less.

Not a man answered Feodor's challenge. Jessie knew what was going through their minds, and didn't greatly blame them. The man who carried the Silver Cane must also be prepared to use it. None were too certain they greatly cared for such an honor—not with the way things were going around the village.

"So, then." Feodor turned to Torgler. "We wait. We do not sell."

Torgler kept his temper, but Jessie could see the red coals of anger burning just behind his eyes. "It is your choice, of course," he said evenly. He spoke to Feodor, but looked straight at Jessie. "Perhaps you'll change your mind, and we can talk again. I will look forward to that time."

"If we do, you will hear of it," Feodor said bluntly. He hadn't missed Torgler's unspoken message, and didn't much care for it. "Now, please leave. This land does not belong to you!"

Torgler turned on his heel and stalked calmly to his horse, as if he owned the village already and all its people. Once mounted, however, he could control his temper no longer. He gave his horse such a savage kick that it danced away over the common and showed the whites of its eyes, then bolted out of the settlement. Jessie walked up beside Feodor and they watched Torgler ride away toward Roster.

"He's not through with us. You know that, don't you?"

"Yes, I know. I know what I have done here today."

"Do you? Do you, Feodor?" Sonia swept past Jessie, her face flushed in anger. "How could you *do* that to him? You have shamed him before his people. I—I will never forgive you. Never!"

"Sonia—"

Tears blurred her eyes and she bit her lip. She stared at Feodor a long moment, struggled to find words, then turned and ran for her father. Gustolf was standing alone, staring out at nothing. Sonia put her arm around him and guided him into the house. The big, blustering man with the fiercely determined eyes had disappeared. In his place, Jessie saw a man who'd crumbled in upon himself, shrunk within his clothes—as if the younger man had somehow sucked all the power out of his frame and taken it for his own.

"I know what it took to do that," said Jessie, catching the look in Feodor's eyes. "I don't know any other way you could have done it."

"I could have not done it at all."

"I don't think that's true, Feodor."

"No." He shrugged his shoulders and looked at her. "It's not, Jessica. It had to be done. And there was no one else to do it."

Jessie sighed and walked with him past the common. "Torgler won't sit still, you can count on that. If he backs down now—damn!" She blew a quick breath between her teeth and impatiently studied the horizon. "I hope Ki gets that girl. I don't much care for Lucy Jordan, but she's sure not a fool. If Ki brings her back, she's got enough sense to know there's not a lawyer in the country—Torgler included—who can talk her out of this one. Unless I'm mistaken, she'll be ripe for talking to me or anyone else who can keep her head out of a noose." She turned to Feodor. "Ki will bring her here because he knows that's where I'll be. She might even have something to say that will help convince your people what's going on."

Feodor looked hopeful, then screwed up his face. "Maybe. I'm not certain they'd believe *anything*, Jessica. Even if they saw it."

Jessie stopped him and smiled. "Hey. *You* got them started, friend. Some of these people are thinking pretty hard now."

Feodor stopped before a door to one of the cottages. "Would you come in for some wine? Oh, of course if you—"

"What?" Jessie gave him a saucy grin. "If I'm worried about who sees me going into a man's cabin? I'm not, Feodor. I *do* care what people think. Sometimes, anyway. What they're thinking, though, usually doesn't have much to do with what's real."

Feodor gave her a bold, appraising look, from her coppery blonde hair to the tips of her boots. "If you come into *this* man's cabin, Jessica Starbuck, what they *think* will have a good deal to do with what's going on."

"Now *that* sounds worth looking into," Jessie said lightly. "What do you think'll happen to me in there?"

"Your worst fears come true," Feodor promised. "Only the worst."

"Sounds truly awful," said Jessie. "Never know for sure till I try, will I?"

Feodor's small cottage was nearly empty. There was a bed, a crude table, and two chairs; a blanket was hung

151

across the far end of the room. If Gustolf's dark furniture and somber tapestries were reminders of the Old World, Feodor's stark surroundings were more typical of the new. It was the room of a man who'd bet all his chips on the future, on what his hands could wrest out of the land.

He sat down beside her on the bed and frowned at the wall. "What do you think he will do, Jessie?"

"Torgler, you mean? Just what he's been doing, if you want my best guess. It's worked pretty well so far, hasn't it?"

"Oh, quite well indeed," Feodor said soberly. *"Damn* the man!" He ground his teeth and dug his big fists into his knees. "What did I accomplish out there, Jessica? Besides crushing an old man I love dearly? If a wolf returns to this place tonight, who is going to care that I stood up to this Torgler? They will not believe that he is behind the thing. Not in a hundred years."

"You had to do it," Jessie reminded him. "You know that. And it's not over, Feodor. It's not. We can beat him!"

Feodor stared. "If a wolf comes and takes another life? Is this how we will beat him, Jessica?"

Jessie had no answer. Instead, she reached up and curled her arms strongly about his neck and drew his mouth down to meet her own. Feodor responded with a fierce, desperate need. There was none of the gentle lovemaking he and Jessie had experienced on the banks of the creek. Feodor took her hard and used her, tore her out of her clothes and plunged himself inside her. Jessie gave him as good as she got. Her long legs scissored about his back and welcomed him in. Her teeth dug hungrily into his shoulder and her nails raked his flesh. When they reached the heights of their pleasure, they both cried out. Feodor filled her with his warmth, and Jessie joyously opened her body to let him in...

★

Chapter 16

The sun passed over the low hills, and the narrow tunnel of trees became gray and indistinct. The creek turned to a ribbon of dark water, its banks lost in shadow. Ki stopped warily, all his senses strained to catch the slightest hint of danger. Reason told him to run, to flee the tangled woods and bolt quickly into the open where he could see an enemy coming. It took all the samurai discipline he could muster to stand his ground.

Only moments before, the waning light had swallowed the trail he'd followed. Even when he bent close to the ground, there was nothing, and he dared not risk a match to check for sign. Logically, Zascha and the horses should still be up ahead—keeping to the relatively clear path above the creek, out of the trees. Logic, though, would not save his life if he was wrong—if the hunter had left his mounts and doubled back, if he was waiting along the creek, his finger on the trigger . . .

Ki cast that thought aside. Unless he'd read the trail wrong, Zascha wasn't even thinking about him anymore. Something had put the fear of God into the man and he was running for his life. The earlier sign had made that clear—the wolf tracks, and those others, the enormous prints of the...*creature* who ran with those beasts...

When the idea came to him, he carried it out at once, without a second thought. Leaving the dark trees, he slipped quietly down into the creek. Almost immediately, he felt a great sense of relief, as if some terrible burden had been lifted off his shoulders. He had regained some control over his surroundings. The sound of shallow water masked his movements, and he could see a fair distance in every direction. Whatever came at him, he would at least have a few seconds' warning.

The water was knee-deep at most, and his bare feet found solid footing on the gravelly bottom. Ki moved quietly down the stream, stopping every few yards to listen and test the air. He had been in the creek only moments before he smelled it. When it struck his senses, he froze, every muscle and tendon taut as a wire.

Animal! Just a slight hint on the wind, but it was enough, and unmistakable. Wild, musty, rank...a raw, sickly sweet odor that was there, and then suddenly gone. Ki smelled his own sweat, and prayed that whatever was out there had missed the scent. It was close, *too* close...

A high, ragged shriek pierced the night, hung on the air a long moment, then cut off abruptly. Ki crouched in the water and jerked the *sai* from his belt. Another sound instantly covered the first. The low, throaty growl of a wolf. No—more than one! Then—six quick shots as someone emptied a revolver. A horse screamed in pain and a man shouted in fear. Hooves thundered off, crashing wildly through the brush. And after that—nothing.

Ki didn't move. His eyes swept the darkness. His sensitive ears searched for sound in the sudden, awful silence. Once he thought he heard something snuffling on the bank over his head. Sweat coursed down his brow and stung his eyes. He could almost see the great wolf crouching there, ready to spring.

154

It seemed like forever before his senses allowed him to move. He knew he couldn't stand there all night like a statue, but it seemed like a fair idea. Moving one foot carefully before the other, he walked a good twenty yards upstream, then stepped onto the shore. He listened another long moment, then silently made his way up the bank.

He could smell it before he even reached the top, and knew what it was. The terrible odor of death. The coppery smell of blood. The choking smell of bowels loosed in fear . . .

He found the horse first. It lay in a slight depression twenty feet from the creek. Its belly was split wide, and the pearly coils that had spilled out glistened in the dim light. A few feet away he found the man. Most of his head was gnawed and slashed away. He knew it was Zascha from the man's great size and the European rifle still clutched in his fist.

Ki felt a quick moment of anger. He had wanted this one himself—wanted to meet him out here in the dark, one against the other. Settling things up for Lucy Jordan was *his* business, and the wolves had cheated him of that.

There was nothing more to learn, and he felt decidedly uncomfortable, vulnerable, and open. After a quick look around, he snatched up Zascha's rifle and hurried off through the trees, away from the creek, into the grasslands beyond. Crouching on his heels, he took deep breaths till his pulse slowed to normal. Thinking back, he put the picture together as well as he could. The death cry. Zascha, for certain. And Zascha's horse. The others, his and Lucy's, had bolted through the trees and would likely never stop until they dropped. But that wasn't the whole of it. There was *another* man out here—the one who'd shouted and emptied his pistol. If the wolves had gotten him too, his body would've been nearby. He couldn't get away on foot, so he still had a horse. Who was he? Ki wondered. What was he doing with Zascha?

It didn't matter. Whoever he was, he was long gone now

if he had any sense. Ki shrugged, stood, and started off up the hill in an easy run. It was still a long way to the village. With any luck at all, he could get there in time to warn the settlers that they could expect more visitors. Maybe they'd believe him when he told them one of their own was involved.

Ki came to a sudden halt and stared down the hill. The horse lay belly up, twisting its legs in pain. The man was running frantically up the low rise beyond, plowing a drunken path through the grass. As Ki topped the hill, the man paused, looked wildly over his shoulder, and saw Ki watching. A ragged cry escaped his lips and he staggered back in fear, caught himself, and tore through the grass, screaming and waving his arms.

Ki ran along the crest, then angled down the valley. He narrowed the distance between them without effort, clutched a handful of collar, and tossed his prey to the ground.

The man howled, rolled in the grass, and kicked his feet. His clothes were ripped and he was covered with dirt and blood. Still, Ki decided, any man who had this much energy was not hurt badly.

"Stop it," he said shortly. "Be still and let me see what's wrong with you."

The man turned pale at Ki's voice, jerked his knees up under his chin, and covered his face.

"Don't hurt me don't hurt me oh Jesus don't hurt me!" His cries were the high-pitched pleas of a frightened child. Ki stood back, shook his head, and grinned.

"I won't," he said flatly. "I wouldn't hurt you for the world."

Jessie stood against the wall of the cottage and peered into the dark. The sun had died quickly, and the night seemed to rush in to smother the earth. Even the cold stars and a bright full moon were masked by swiftly moving clouds. Jessie was grateful for the small fires circling the village. They were pitifully few, but better than nothing. At least

156

they might give the settlement a few moments' warning.

Even as Jessie watched, a fire past the last cottage in the village flared quickly, then faded to embers. Footsteps sounded in the dark and Jessie gripped her Colt, then recognized Feodor and relaxed.

"Another fire is gone, yes?" he growled. "You don't have to tell me." His dark features clouded with anger and frustration. "By *God,* Jessica. They have all left me—every one of them. Crept behind their doors like old grandmothers." He looked at the cane in his fist and gave a harsh little laugh. "Now I know what an elder is for. He does everything no one else wants to do!"

"You can't get *any* of them to stand up with you? Not one, Feodor?"

"No. Not one." He gave her a long, weary look. "It is too much for them, Jessie. They have centuries behind them in the Old World—two years in this one."

"I wish Ki were here. He could help, and—" She stopped and looked into the dark. "I'm worried about him, Feodor. I think he'd try to get back here before dark, whether he found Lucy Jordan or not."

"He is a good man. He will be all right." He stepped close to Jessie and held her. "You will fight me, but it is no use arguing. I want you inside. Now."

"Oh, *wait* just a minute!" Jessie flared.

"No." He raised a big palm to cut her off. "It is settled. There is too much danger out here."

"But it's all right for you, huh?"

"I am a—"

"You finish that sentence with *man,* Feodor, and you're going to wish a pack of wolves would take my place!"

Feodor laughed. "You are a stubborn, impossible woman."

"Oh?" Jessie's green eyes flashed. "That isn't what you said a while ago. You said I was *very* cooperative, that I drove you absolutely crazy and you loved it."

"That has nothing to do with this."

"Feodor..." Jessie's voice softened. "I know what

157

you're trying to do and I appreciate it. Only I don't figure on being just a lover in bed. If I can lie down with you, I can do my part standing up, too." She gave him a quick little smile. "It's not as if you've got any choice, you know."

Feodor let out a breath. "I don't know why I even bother."

"Well, I do. Because you're—My God! What's that?"

Feodor dropped the silver cane and snatched up a Winchester leaning against the wall. "Move over to the left and cover me," he snapped. "Keep low and close to the cabin!"

Jessie nodded and Feodor ran off into the dark. The shadowy figure moved toward him from the direction of the creek. No—there were *two* of them! Gray, indistinct forms against the lowering clouds. Jessie's hair stood on end as she steadied the Colt in her fist. The figures swam before her eyes, took on ungodly shapes...

"Hold it!" shouted Feodor. "Right there!"

"I'll be glad to," said a familiar voice out of the dark. "I'm very tired of running."

"Ki!" Jessie cried out with joy, and ran down to meet him. Walking out of the high grass, he shoved the other man before him and sent him sprawling.

"I ran across a friend," he said evenly. "I'm sure you will be pleased to see him again, Jessie."

"What?" Jessie took a step back and stared. *Torgler!* Now where in hell did *he* come from!"

"It's a very long story." Ki shook hands with Feodor and gripped Jessie warmly. "I have much to tell you, and so does he, I'm certain." He gave Torgler a dark look and pulled him to his feet. "Can we get inside somewhere? I could use a cup of coffee."

Feodor exchanged a quick look with Jessie. "Whatever this is, I want Gustolf to hear. Whether I am welcome there or not."

"What?" Ki looked puzzled.

"Never mind," said Jessie. That's a long story too."

* * *

Gustolf reacted as Feodor had expected, and tried to slam the door in his face. Feodor ignored him and shoved his way inside, dragging the disheveled Torgler behind him. Gustolf took one look at the man and shrank back in disbelief.

"The creature has struck again—it is back!" He shot an accusing finger at Feodor. "You see what you have done? I knew it!"

"You do *not* know," Feodor said bluntly. "But this man knows a great deal. Sonia, would you see to his wounds? He is not badly hurt, but he needs help."

Sonia gave him a dark look, but hurried to fetch rags and water.

"What—what is all this?" Gustolf demanded. "It is plain what has happened here. I do not need you to tell me!"

"I think that you do," Ki said wearily. He wanted to drop in a chair and stay there, but stood his ground and faced the old man. "I followed Lucy Jordan from Roster and caught her at the old way station." He glanced quickly at Jessie. "She's dead," he said flatly. "A wolf tore her throat out."

"Oh, *no!*" Jessie put a hand to her breast.

"The wolf is dead too, Gustolf. Lucy killed it. And not with a silver bullet."

Gustolf's eyes narrowed. "I do not believe that. You are lying."

"Damn it, I don't care *what* you believe!" Ki could hold back his feelings no longer. His dark eyes blazed with such fury that even Jessie was taken aback. "Try this, old man, and see how you like it. The man responsible for all these so-called werewolves was one of your own. Zascha! Now his pets have turned on him—he's dead back there on the creek." He jerked up the rifle he'd been holding by his side and threw it at Gustolf's feet.

"No . . ." Gustolf stared at the weapon and shook his head. "This is—not so!"

"It is," Feodor said shortly. "Believe the man, Gustolf.

159

For God's sake, come to your senses!"

"Believe him!" Gustolf went rigid and trembled all over. "He is not one of us—he accuses one of our own of this horror, and you ask me to believe him?"

"Believe *him,* then," said Ki. He walked over and grasped Torgler's shoulder until he winced. "Tell him. Now. We will hear your part in this. All of it."

"Leave him alone," Sonia flared angrily. "The man is hurt!"

"Not yet, he isn't."

Torgler looked about wildly, his eyes darting from one side of the room to the other. "I—I don't know what you're talking about. I don't know anything!"

"You know a great deal about wolves," prompted Ki. "That would be a good place to start."

"I was attacked," Torgler blurted. "Good God, man, you can see that. I left here for Roster and—"

"You did what?" Jessie raised a brow. "Torgler, you left here right after noon. You could've ridden to Roster and back half a dozen times!"

"I—" Torgler bit his lip. "The—the creatures were after me. They got on my trail as soon as I left, and I couldn't shake them off. That's the truth!"

Ki started for him. Feodor held him back and shot him a look. "We are wasting time. If the man does not wish to answer questions, he does not have to."

"Now look!" shouted Ki. Relief flooded Torgler's features.

Feodor jerked him out of the chair by the collar. "Get out. Now."

"What?" Torgler's mouth fell open. "I don't—"

"There is nothing to discuss here. You are free. Get out of the village." Feodor dragged him to the door and opened it. Torgler suddenly understood what was happening to him.

"Nooooo!" he shrieked, writhing against Feodor's grip. "You—you *can't!"* He glanced fearfully at Jessie. "Don't let him do this. Please!"

Jessie shrugged. "I don't think it's legal," she said soberly, "but he's the elder here. Nothing much I can do." She gave Torgler a reassuring smile. "I *will* ride into town in the morning and see if I can get you a good lawyer."

"A—" Torgler paled. Feodor let him go and he sank feebly back in the chair. His shoulders sagged and he buried his face in his hands.

"All right," he muttered, "I knew about it—"

"No!" bellowed Feodor. He jerked the man up again and slammed him down hard. "Tell it, all of it, you bastard, or by God you go out there!"

Torgler shrank away from him, and gripped the arm of his chair to keep from shaking. "All right. I—I hired Zascha. He—worked for me—"

"He brought the wolves in when you told him to," Jessie finished. "You ordered him to kill here at the settlement, so you could scare these folks off their land. And you used the animals again to get rid of Gaiter."

"Yes—*yes!*" moaned Torgler.

"Great Jesus Christ! A man could do this thing?" Gustolf came at him, his face twisted in rage. It was all Ki could do to hold him back.

"Go on," Feodor prompted. "The rest of it. You are not finished yet."

"That other man out there," Ki demanded sharply. "Who is he? I saw his tracks."

Jessie looked up, startled. "What are you talking about, Ki?"

"He knows. He'll tell us."

Torgler bit his lip and looked away. "Zascha didn't train the wolves—or control them. God, no one could do that...no one who wasn't...." He stopped and let out a breath. "Some of my people found him. In the Nebraska hills, I think. He's a mountain man, wild as an animal. The wolves belong to him. He's an enormous hulk of a man— a giant. Only he has the mind of a child—never lived with another human. Just his wolves—they're bigger than any I've ever seen..."

Ki glanced quickly at Jessie, and she knew who she'd

161

seen, stalking out under the moon.

"Only Zascha could get near him," Torgler went on. "He could talk to him somehow—make him understand. We had him tell the man that if he'd"—Torgler caught Gustolf's eyes and looked away—"that if he'd help drive your people off the land, we'd give him a place of his own. Somewhere no one would bother him and his damn wolves..." Torgler paused. "I—don't know. There's nothing more..."

Ki stepped up, reached out, and forced Torgler to look at him. "What happened out there tonight? Why did this maniac turn his wolves on you and Zascha?"

"We promised none of the animals would be harmed," sighed Torgler.

"And one of them was," said Ki. "When Lucy killed it, the man went berserk, right?"

"Yes—that's what happened. He has six of the animals. Five now." Torgler squeezed to his eyes shut. "He—set the things on us. I was supposed to leave here and meet Zascha later..." He seemed reluctant to go on, and Ki knew why.

"Before you left town, you sent word to Zascha to be sure Lucy didn't get away alive."

"Or Ki either, if he was around," added Jessie.

Torgler nodded. "Lucy knew the old stage stop. So did Zascha. We met there sometimes. The crazy old man keeps his wolves about six miles up in the hills from there."

We don't need to ask why you and Zascha were meeting," Feodor said darkly. "When I wouldn't sell today, you planned to send them in again. Tonight."

Torgler wouldn't look at him. "He won't send in just one—not now. He'll bring all of them. And this time, he'll come with them."

★

Chapter 17

"This time we will be ready for them," Feodor said through gritted teeth. "This time—" He stopped and glanced savagely at Gustolf. "Do you see what we are? What they think of us? This man who would steal our land knew we would not even try to kill the beasts! We were too frightened, too sure of our ways. They had nothing but contempt for us, Gustolf. And by the living saints, they were right!"

Gustolf colored, but his anger was directed at Torgler now, not at Feodor. "This is so, eh? You answer!"

"Yes—*yes!*" Torgler flinched and shrank back in his chair. "I've—told you the whole thing, damn it!"

"You got Zascha to work for you? Zascha? Why does he do this? Tell me that!"

For a moment it was the haughty, self-assured man Jessie remembered who spoke to Gustolf. "Same reason as all the others," he said wryly. "Money. Power. And not a lot, at that." Torgler almost smiled. "Men know their worth, sir. And they place damn little value on themselves."

"Shut up!" Feodor shook a big fist in Torgler's face. "I have heard all I care to hear from your mouth." He lifted

163

the man up, threw him against the door, and turned to Gustolf. "Will you help me? Go with me to tell the others what we know?"

Gustolf closed his eyes, then opened them again and faced the younger man. "Yes." He said finally. "I will. I will go, and we will take this thing that calls itself a man along with us."

Feodor grinned. "I would not let him out of my sight. Not for a moment." He gripped Torgler's arm so hard the man paled. "Come, my friend. Our people were greatly impressed with you this morning. I would have them see you again."

Gustolf stopped to gather up a lantern, and instructed Sonia to fill the others as quickly as she could, as many as she could find. Sonia protested, but Gustolf insisted she stay in the cabin until he returned. Feodor opened the door and shoved Torgler out into the night. Jessie and Ki joined him, and Gustolf followed. After a few steps, Jessie held back and stopped Ki.

"I think we ought to let them handle this," she told him. "You and I haven't done all that well convincing people lately."

"Yes, I can't argue with that."

Jessie looked at him. "You had kind of a tough time out there, didn't you? I'm sorry, Ki. And I don't mind telling you I was worried."

Ki grinned wearily. "Thank you, Jessie. And yes. There were—difficulties."

"Oh, well, if that's all . . ." She raised one eyebrow and made a noise. "Difficulties, huh? You look like someone put you through a wringer."

"Someday you will spoil me with your flattery."

"Yeah, but you'll get over it." She studied him a minute and decided what was wrong. "Your hat. You don't have it on."

"I lost it. Out there somewhere."

"Oh," she said solemnly, "I'm sorry to hear that. It was

a real fine hat. Couldn't have been more than ten or fifteen years old."

"Not quite. It was well broken in, though. I doubt I'll find another half as good."

"That sure would take some doing," Jessie agreed. She started to speak again, but something told her to keep her silence. There'd been something in his eyes when he spoke. Lucy Jordan? she wondered, and instantly knew she was right. Ki and Lucy. Something had happened out there. It was more than Lucy's dying, though that was certainly a part of it. Ki would keep his pain to himself, she knew, and lick his own wounds. That had always been his way.

Ki stopped suddenly and listened. "Ah, there!" He motioned toward the fields. "They are here now, Jessie."

"Did you hear them?"

"No," he said evenly. "There is a light wind, and I can smell them. I have learned more than I care to about wolves. Feodor—" Ki glanced once more into the darkness and trotted toward the open door of a cottage. Several men were clustered around Gustolf in a pool of yellow light. Feodor turned at Ki's voice, and Ki pulled him aside. "They're here," he announced. "Not far, either. Out in the wheat. Probably coming in from the creek side, too. I don't know how much control this wild man has over his creatures."

"Enough, I'm sure." Feodor made a face and nodded over his shoulder. "I was too optimistic. Even Gustolf can't convince them, though Torgler is cooperating nicely. He's more frightened of the old man than he is of me or the wolves."

"That old man can be rather frightening," said Ki. He stepped into the light next to Gustolf.

"Here—ask this man!" Gustolf said expansively. He pounded Ki on the shoulder. "He has seen the wolf die. He knows!"

One of the men studied Ki suspiciously and rattled off a long garble of speech. Gustolf curled his lip in contempt. "Bah!" He spat at the man's feet and made him jump. "He says that is all very well, but he does not know you and therefore cannot know exactly what you have seen."

"A nice way of saying I'm lying."

Gustolf forced a grin. "It is. We are a very tactful people. Stubborn sometimes, but nearly always polite."

"Fine," said Ki. "That won't help much if we—"

His words were lost as a terrible cry cut through the darkness—the deep, resonant howl of a wolf. Almost immediately, another took up the call, then another and another, until the summer night was filled with the chilling sound.

The settlers who were gathered about Gustolf went rigid. "He is here!" one gasped. "The man-wolf has come!"

"No!" blurted Ki. "They're *wolves,* damn it! That's *all* they are. You shoot them and they die like anything else!"

The settlers looked at Ki as if he were crazy. One broke and ran for his cottage. It was all the others needed. Gustolf threatened and shook his fist. Feodor stood his ground and cursed them, but the men tore past him and disappeared.

"Stay together," Ki shouted. He pulled Jessie to him and swept his eyes over the darkness. "Gustolf—take the lantern and hold it up high. We've got to have light!"

Feodor levered a shell into his rifle and backed up against Ki. "We can't stay out here. We can stop one, perhaps, but if they come at us in a pack—"

"I don't think we've got much choice," said Jessie. "We're not going to make it to your place, Gustolf. And no one's going to open a door to us now. Ki, can you—" Jessie stopped as someone screamed, slammed her to the ground, and rushed past her.

"Torgler!" Ki shouted. "Get back here!"

Torgler couldn't hear him. He ran a few yards, jerked to a stop, and started aimlessly in another direction.

"Oh, no!" Jessie pulled herself to her feet as the man circled wildly about the common, shouting something she couldn't understand.

"Goddamn fool!" snorted Gustolf. "Doesn't know what he's—"

"Torgler—look out!" Feodor dropped to his knees and fired into the darkness. The flash from his muzzle threw the wolf's shadow against a cabin wall. Torgler turned, too late—Feodor emptied his rifle into the night and came to his feet.

"Damn! There's nothing there—nothing!"

"There was," Jessie assured him. "You hit him—just not good enough."

A snarl of anger came from the hollow, and turned them all around. Something moved quickly past one of the dying fires, and Jessie caught a glimpse of red eyes and flashing teeth.

"There!" Ki pointed just behind the animal. "Another one. There are two of them now."

Feodor cursed and slid new shells into his Winchester, spilling half of them on the ground. Jessie leveled her Colt and fired twice. One of the beasts yelped and both disappeared.

"You are right," said Gustolf. "We cannot stay out here, Feodor. They are clever—and too fast!"

Ki caught the tremor in the old man's voice. "We'll be all right if we stick together," he said calmly. "Keep against the wall and keep moving. At least we don't have to cover our backs."

"Lafka—damn your soul—open!" Gustolf beat his fists on the door of the house whose wall they were hugging, his face purple with rage. "This is on *my* head," he said tightly. "Mine, no one else's. I have brought us all to this!"

"You believed what you were taught to believe." Feodor grasped his shoulder. "All of us have, Gustolf. For too long now."

Jessie spotted something at the edge of the common, and fired. A shadow moved swiftly away. Ki led them to the end of the cabin. The next was only a few yards away, but

167

the darkness between them seemed to stretch out for miles. Ki looked warily around the corner and turned to the others.

"I would like very much to be inside, but I see no reason to risk going further. If we can't put a door behind us, we are as well off here as anyplace else."

"Funny, I don't *feel* well off," muttered Jessie. The night seemed filled with ghostly shapes. Everywhere she looked, something moved—shadow against shadow. The butt of the Colt felt reassuring in her hand. It was hard to keep from firing into the dark, spraying lead to bolster her courage. If we don't get out of this fast, that'll happen, she told herself grimly. We'll be facing those creatures with a couple of empty guns...

"The two that showed up by the creek have moved in closer," Feodor whispered. "They're behind those cabins across the common."

"That only leaves three, if Torgler's right."

"Only?"

Jessie forced a grin. "Doesn't sound right, does it? Look, if they come we'll—God, what's that!"

A high-pitched wail cut through the night. Ki froze in his tracks. "That wasn't a wolf!"

"No..." Jessie's heart leaped up in her throat. "Oh, Lord, Ki, look—it's a *child!*"

"That can't be!" said Feodor.

"There!" Jessie gripped his arm and pointed. "Past that second cottage."

"You're jumping at shadows," he told her. "I don't see a—*Jessie,* no!"

Jessie didn't let herself think. She held the Colt loosely in her hand and ran low, keeping one eye on the small white figure, the other on the darkness closing in from every side. The child saw her, and looked up with frightened eyes.

"Jessie, look out!"

Feodor and Ki shouted at once. Jessie heard the throaty growl at her heels, and scooped up the child without stopping. A Winchester exploded behind her. Jessie risked a look over her shoulder. The wolf snarled and bit at the air, dancing in the hail of lead. She had a second or two, maybe—no more than that. She hefted the child in her arms and tossed it at the low, sod-covered roof, then hoisted herself up behind. The child fell past her, screaming as it rolled back toward the edge. Jessie caught it by the leg, turned on her back, and saw the wolf leap off the ground straight for her. She brought the Colt up fast, and fired three quick shots at the animal's chest. The wolf howled and clawed past her, snapping its jaws to try and kill her as it died. Jessie cried out and jerked away, clutching the child to her. She felt herself slipping, tried to dig her heels through the roof, and tumbled to the ground. Jessie took the blow herself, holding the child up high. The pistol flew out of her hand. Sucking in air to fill her lungs, she sat up shakily and scrambled for the Colt, brushing the ground frantically in the dark.

The sound brought her around and froze the blood in her veins. The creature came at her, head low to the ground, white teeth bared in a deathly grin. There was no time left, and she knew it. Out of the corner of her eye she saw Ki running toward her, and knew he'd never reach her. The wolf tossed its head, tensed its hard body, and leaped—

Yellow fire blossomed. Twin peals of thunder roared across the common. The wolf's head exploded, spattering Jessie with blood. She turned in disbelief and saw the young woman in the doorway, the shotgun cradled in her arms. Very calmly she broke open the weapon, digging in her apron for new shells.

"Jessie—you all right?"

"I—guess so." Ki helped her up. Jessie searched for her Colt and found it. A woman cried out, ran toward them, and drew the bawling child into her arms. Tears filled her eyes. Her thanks rushed out in words Jessie couldn't understand, but the meaning was clear enough.

"Is the one I got—dead?" asked Jessie. "I got it, didn't I?"

"Yes. You got it," Ki said dryly. He felt as if he'd aged a hundred years in the last two minutes. "It came very close to getting *you*."

"Yeah, I noticed."

"Good. Next time, Jessie—"

Feodor bellowed across the common, pointing frantically to his left. Ki saw them at once, and raised a hand to hold Jessie back. Two gray shadows bounded into the clearing, fur raised high on their backs. Jessie checked her Colt, stepped to the right, and saw Feodor back off slowly, bringing the Winchester to his shoulder.

"Don't move," Ki said beside her. "Stay perfectly still."

A door jerked open behind Jessie. She nearly jumped out of her skin. A stout settler walked out, hesitated a moment, and took a bold step forward, a large piece of firewood clutched in a callused hand. A woman in a long gown came up behind him, gripping a poker from the fire. A door past Feodor added its own pool of light to the common. A gaunt, gray-haired man as old as Gustolf walked over his doorstep, brandishing a wicked, three-pronged pitchfork.

Jessie gripped Ki's arm. A chill touched the back of her neck. Feodor's people appeared like ghosts, grimly filling the common until they ringed the beasts in a circle. The two wolves backed cautiously away, cold eyes sweeping the crowd. One pawed the ground, snarled, and snapped at the air. They were wary, bewildered. Whatever was happening here was outside their experience. Every instinct told them to spring, but something held them back...

The crowd moved in. Several men had torches, and now they held them high, waving the licking flames at the wolves. Light banished shadow and made the animals real...

Jessie saw that there were few guns among the villagers. For the most part, they clutched the tools they worked with—forks, picks, axes, and sharp-bladed scythes. She knew it mattered little what they carried. Anger and pride were their real weapons, and they were learning how to use

170

them. Her eyes swept the circle and stopped. It was the woman with the shotgun who'd saved her life, and Jessie realized with a start who she was—the young widow of Michael Antonescu, the man who'd been killed the night she arrived.

Across the circle, she saw Feodor step up to Gustolf and press the Winchester into his hands. The old man looked at him a long moment, then a grim smile crossed his features. More had passed between them than a rifle, Jessie knew. Gustolf levered a shell into the chamber and glanced proudly at Sonia by his side. Then he raised the rifle quickly and fired, worked the lever, and fired once more. A shotgun roared, and an old pistol boomed. A pitchfork flashed in the light and plunged into the center of the circle. An ax caught the glint of a torch. Gustolf bellowed, and the crowd took up his cry. Jessie turned away from the sight. The wolves didn't need more killing—but Gustolf's people did.

Feodor caught Jessie's eye, took a dozen long strides, and swept her into his arms.

"It is over," he grinned. "All but one. And we'll get him too, by God. And his crazy keeper as well!"

"You can be proud of them," said Jessie.

"Ah, I am, I am! Better than that, they are proud of themselves." A shadow crossed his face, and he clutched her shoulders tightly. "That was a brave thing you did. No one here will forget it. For a minute I thought you were—" Feodor clamped his jaws and didn't finish.

Jessie laughed and pulled away. "So did Ki, but I'm not. I think I scared him more than I've ever—" She stopped, suddenly turned away, and frantically searched the common. "Ki. Oh, my God, Feodor!" A tremor coursed through her body as she clutched a hand to her breast. "He's out there. He went out after that wild man by himself!"

★

Chapter 18

He knew they were there ...

The night was far different from that other, when he had first followed Gustolf into the fields. Then he'd found it hard to wear the skin of his enemy, to become the wolf itself. The beast had nearly fooled him, cunningly shifting its fury to the hapless old man.

He no longer searched for sign, a faint hint of odor on the wind. Now the *kime* of the beast was all around him. It was a thickness in the air, a heavy, brutal presence that assaulted his senses. So many wolves had prowled the high wheat, he was blind to the one he sought.

He was far from the village now, deep into the endless sea of wheat. The field murmured and sighed. Dark clouds swept so low to the earth, he could almost hear them whisper.

They are close now ... and they know that I am here ...

He stopped and stood perfectly still, projecting his senses into the night, casting the delicate web and waiting to see where it touched. They were bearing to the left, out of the fields, toward the trees that masked the creek. The man and the wolf were together, moving steadily away from his path.

Ki came suddenly alert. Something he couldn't name pricked the edge of his senses.

They are running, but not retreating, and that is not the same thing . . . they are waiting for me . . . drawing me in . . .

He pictured where he was in his mind, and drew a mental arrow toward the creek along the path of the wolf and its keeper. Then he drew a second line, slightly below and to the left. With luck and a fast pace, it would take him to the creek before the others . . .

Ki slid quietly down the bank of the creek, exactly as he had done earlier that night, some miles farther upstream. Moving slowly through the water, he brought his breath under control, slowed the beat of his heart, and buried his fears under a curtain of serenity and peace.

The man and the wolf were up there. They were searching for him now along the banks, and back the way they'd come through the fields. The keeper kept to the trees and sent the wolf ranging ahead. Ki could sense its presence, almost see it in his mind as it loped silently through the dark, muzzle low to the ground, fiery red eyes searching every leaf and stone in its path. It had missed him so far because the high banks and the water masked his scent. Soon, though, it would discover where he'd entered the water and return with this news to its master. When that happened, Ki knew he had to be gone. The creek was a useful passage and nothing more. It was not a fighting ground. He didn't dare let them catch him there . . .

Ki froze, trying to become one with the night. The wolf was close—close—*close!* So near he could almost hear the beast's soft pads upon the earth, smell the wild odor of its fur.

He knew he could wait no longer. The wolf had told the man. The man knew, and he was coming—bounding through the woods with a terrible rage in his heart.

Ki scrambled up the bank and flattened himself against a tall tree. He gripped one of the razor-edged *shuriken* in each hand. The star-shaped disks of steel felt as natural to his touch as the flesh of his body. In a sense, they truly *were* extensions of himself. Ki had spent a great part of his life learning to kill. Now the weapons he used were merely hands with other shapes.

Silently he moved away from the tree and searched the dark. Clouds still covered the moon. No light at all filtered through the branches above...

Suddenly it was there, a gray shadow loping through the brush, moving toward him like a specter without a sound. Ki bent his knees, let the breath sigh out of his lungs. The fear was still with him, bound like a prisoner behind the paper-thin wall of his thoughts.

A moment...a small moment more...now!

Ki controlled his fear no longer. It welled up within him, surging through his veins and chilling his blood...It sought him out to bring him to his knees, but Ki embraced it like a brother, gripped it in his hands like a sword.

The wolf instinctively sensed the sudden change in its victim...it smelled the stink of terror unleashed by the man-thing...its primitive heart sang out with murderous joy, and even as it bounded off the ground, stretched to rip the man-thing's throat, its dark brain whispered that this was no danger at all, no more than a hare in the fields...

"Heeeeeee-hai!" The sharp cry burst from Ki's lungs.

The razored metal stars left his hands in a blur, hummed across the night, and tore the flesh of the wolf. The animal howled and jerked its head in pain. Ki stepped deftly aside, felt the wolf's foul breath on his shoulder, heard its body snap branches and tumble into the creek.

Quickly he dismissed the wolf from his mind. He knew where the *shuriken* had struck, for he knew where his hands had sent them—one to the throat, the other between the eyes. The second missile had sliced through bone and cut well into the brain.

He had no time for a dead foe now—there was another enemy somewhere about, this one likely as dangerous as

175

the first. Two more stars were already in his hands. He sprang off to the right, moving as far from the scene as he could. The wolf-keeper knew where he was—Ki had told him that. He'd be coming right for him, following the—

The man rose up like a stone splitting the earth. Ki slammed one foot to the ground, twisted desperately away, whipped back his arm to loose his weapon. It was too late—much too late—and he knew it. The mountain man bellowed out his anger and crushed Ki to his chest. Great arms drove the breath from his body. Ki lashed out with his feet, but the man simply lifted him off the ground and let him kick air. The grip tightened. Ki struggled to move, but couldn't. Pain screamed in every muscle and tendon. Already, searing white lights whirled in his head. It would be over in a second—he'd pass out and his lungs would collapse. And after that—

He could still move his legs, but they were useless... his body, his hands and arms, were crushed in the terrible vise... there was no use... nothing...

It was getting hard to think... too much effort... Ki stopped trying, let himself fall effortlessly through the thick, syrupy—

"No!"

Something cried out angrily inside him, jarred him back to life... he couldn't see it, but he knew what it was... his *kami,* his spirit... it had come to take him away...

He sent a last desperate message coursing through his body. Nothing answered. His head, his legs, his arms—all gone, all—No! There was something. His *hand.* The fingers of his right hand—they were still there, still free. He flexed them tentatively, let them slide a few inches... there was some kind of clothing... the skin of an animal... and beneath that...

He could feel himself slipping, falling gently through the darkness. With a final effort he grasped the thick, fleshy member and wrenched it with the last of his strength...

The giant howled, threw Ki from him, and bent to clutch

176

the pain between his legs. Ki rolled, sucked in precious air, and shook his head. The man rose up and came for him again. His enormous legs shook the ground. Ki caught a quick glimpse of wild, fiery eyes buried in a thick mat of hair, a tangled beard encrusted with filth. The man growled and lumbered toward him. An arm the size of a tree limb whistled past Ki's head, but he wasn't there. He ducked under the blow, jabbed his hand in fast, and danced away.

The giant stopped and rubbed a fist over his bloodied nose in obvious bewilderment. Nothing had ever struck him before. Rage filled his eyes, and he came at Ki with a vengeance. Ki moved about in a circle, palms up and open. God—the bastard was monstrous! Close to seven feet and as thick-bodied as a grizzly. If he ever caught Ki again, gripped him in those arms...

He patted the pocket of his jacket for the weapons that should be there—but the pocket was torn away, the *shuriken* gone. The giant came at him. Ki backed away. A big fist struck out at his head and Ki jumped to the right, twisted, and slammed his feet at the creature's face. The man howled and staggered back. Ki moved in quickly. The giant hammered Ki's shoulder and smashed him hard against a tree. Ki felt a rib snap, but bit back the pain and struggled to his knees. The man kicked out at his head. Ki moved, took the blow on his arm, and scrambled away through the grass.

Damn—he was incredibly fast for his size! He'd misjudged this enemy badly, and the error had nearly cost him his life. He rolled on the ground, jammed one hand into the earth, and snapped his body like a whip. His left foot hit the mountain man in the groin and doubled him up. Ki came to his feet, whirled, kicked out savagely, and drove his foot into a bearded face. An enormous arm came up out of nowhere, clutched Ki's leg in a grip of iron, and threw him across the clearing.

Ki landed badly—the broken rib hit hard and nearly took him under. The giant kicked him in the belly and sent him flying. Ki rolled away, saw a heavy foot coming down to

177

crush him, and threw himself aside. A big knee hit him on the chin, and Ki spit blood. He shook his head, backed off, and let the giant come again. It took all the courage he could muster to stand his ground. He had to, and he knew it. It was the only way.

The giant howled his anger and swept his fist at Ki in a killing blow. Ki jerked his head away, backed off half a step. Another arm whistled past his shoulder. The man roared his frustration, and opened his arms to crush Ki again.

Ki didn't move. He let the arms come, danced in close, and smelled fetid breath on his cheek. His hands lashed out like pistons, whipped back, and struck the hairy face again and again. The hard edges of his palms pounded the thick throat, drove at the matted face. Bone and cartilage snapped. The man staggered, shook blood from his face. Ki hit him again, snaked his left against the hairy temple like an ax, flexed his right arm like a blade, and drove his stiff fingers at the base of the massive nose. The giant went rigid. A cry stuck in his throat. The bone Ki had driven into his brain cut off his life and he dropped like a tree.

Ki stepped back, took a deep breath, and shook his head in wonder. He knew what his feet and hands could do. He had delivered enough lethal blows to kill a dozen men and more, and the monster had nearly taken him instead. He stood for a moment and gazed at the fallen giant. He had done what he had to, and felt no regrets. But there was no great joy in such a thing, either—no pride for a samurai's soul. The man he'd killed hadn't even known that he *was* a man.

Ki turned and walked toward the creek and didn't look back . . .

★

Chapter 19

Ki opened his eyes and caught Jessie watching him from across the compartment. "That is a most peculiar look," he said. "It must have some significance."

"Oh, it does." Jessie swept back her hair and grinned. 'I was just thinking that's a real fine Stetson. Looks good on you."

"Yes. It is a nice gift, and I appreciate it greatly." Ki cleared his throat and looked at the ceiling. "In time, perhaps it will become more—comfortable."

Jessie made a face. "Ki, you are an ungrateful you-know-what."

"This is true."

"What you *really* mean is, in a few years it'll get dirty, greasy, crusted with dust, and you won't be able to tell what color it is."

Ki smiled. "Ah, now there is a hopeful picture. Thank you."

Jessie laughed and shook her head. She looked out at the country rolling by, then turned to him again, puzzlement crossing her features. "I never did figure that out, you know?"

"Figure what out?"

"How Gaiter shot point-blank at that wolf and missed.

Ki stared. "For God's sake, Jessie!"

"No, really. He hit the animal, I know that. What Torgle had to do was get him a little drunk, I guess. Switch th first three bullets for blanks and leave the others in." Sh tapped her chin thoughtfully with the tip of her finger "That's got to be it. He knew how fast those creatures were And he knew Gaiter couldn't possibly get off more than couple of shots . . ."

"Very reasonable and logical," said Ki.

Jessie looked up at his tone. "Well, that's what happened Do you have any better ideas?"

"The answer is much easier than that, Jessie."

"It is?"

"Yes, surely." He looked at her with a perfectly straigh face. "Five of the wolves were ordinary animals. The sixth the one that killed Gaiter, really *was* a werewolf." K shrugged. "Simple, isn't it?"

Jessie looked at him and groaned. "That's *very* funny I'm sure. Let's make a rule, all right? Wolf jokes are out I don't think I'll ever even like *dogs* again."

Jessie went back to her book, and Ki closed his eyes. In the morning they'd be back in Sarah, Texas, the tow Alex Starbuck had named for his wife. And soon after tha they'd be at the ranch. And then . . .

It was over for the moment. They had stopped the carte again, cut off one of its stingers. But he knew, like Jessie that it was never really over.

The faceless men would know who'd beaten them i Roster. They'd come to town when they heard that Torgle had failed, put the pieces together, and learn what ha happened. Eventually someone would ride out to the set tlement and look for answers there. They'd see it then, the message Jessie had left—a challenge that said Alex Star buck was still very much alive in his daughter.

Feodor had pulled down all the posts that circled the

180

village, torn off the wilted wreaths of wolfsbane, and tossed them aside. All but one. Now, instead of pale blossoms, the single post displayed the skin of a wolf, held there by one of Ki's star-shaped *shuriken* driven solidly into the wood. The cartel knew Jessica's calling-card, and wouldn't miss its meaning.

Ki gazed out the window, and saw his reflection in the glass. For a moment, another face swam over his own.

I am sorry, he said silently. *I am sorry, Lucy Jordan . . .*

She had come into his life for only a moment, burning as fast and fiercely as a prairie fire. And in that incredibly short time, she had reached him more than he could have imagined, glimpsed a thing that even Ki would not allow himself to see.

He glanced at Jessie, then turned quickly away. Perhaps she saw a face in the window as well. He did not let his thoughts linger on that.

It is as it must be, he told her in his mind. *I will live with who you are, Jessie. And who I am, as well . . .*

★

Watch for

LONE STAR
AND THE UTAH KID

fifth novel in the hot new
LONE STAR series from Jove

coming in November!

LONGARM

Explore the exciting Old West with
one of the men who made it wild!

LONGARM

Explore the exciting Old West with one of the men who made it wild!